# MY GUY PROBLEM

## A LOVE LIKE THAT NOVEL

### R.L. KENDERSON

# MY GUY PROBLEM

# ONE

## LYDIA

I STARED at my coworkers on my computer screen and checked the clock on the corner. Our Monday morning meeting had hit the one-hour mark, and I was getting antsy. I hadn't made my daily trip down to Caribou Coffee on the corner for a morning latte yet, and the regular coffee from my kitchen wasn't cutting it.

"All right, everyone," Eve—my boss, the editor in chief of the online magazine *Afterglow*—said. "That's it for today. I'll see you all on Thursday."

I waved at the camera and was just about to leave the online meeting when Eve said, "Oh, Lydia, please stay on for a minute."

"Okay," I agreed as my mind began to race about what my boss would want to speak to me about since she never asked me to stay on after our meetings were finished.

As soon as it was just the two of us, Eve said, "What are you doing the third weekend in July?"

I really wanted to know why she was asking before I answered that, but Eve was too smart.

1

I already knew I didn't have anything planned that far out. It was two months away. But I pretended to check the calendar on my desk anyway. "Nothing."

Eve clapped her hands together and grinned. "Great. I didn't say anything in the meeting today, but Hayley broke her leg and needs surgery."

"Oh no."

Hayley was not my favorite coworker; we were just too different, but I wouldn't want her to suffer through something like a broken leg.

Hayley wrote the fitness column for the magazine and worked out at least once, if not twice, a day. My idea of working out was going for a walk to the bakery to buy myself my favorite cupcake. Basically, I didn't do exercise unless I had an incentive.

"Yes, it's not great. She's having surgery today, and she'll be back with us on Thursday." Eve wiggled her fingers. "It's a good thing her fingers aren't broken, so she can keep working."

I raised my eyebrows. "Yeah, good thing." I shouldn't be surprised that Eve was only worried about the bottom line. "So, what do you need me for?"

"Seeing as Hayley can't do anything but sit in a chair or walk on crutches for the next eight weeks, I need you to do the triathlon this year."

I burst out laughing. I did the advice column Ask Lydia and steered as far away from Hayley's articles as I could. I didn't even read them.

Eve gave me a stern look, and I immediately lost my smile.

"Oh crap, you're not joking."

"No, I am not."

"But I don't work out, Eve. I don't even know what a triathlon entails." Biking and running I thought were two of three activities. I *loathed* running. "There has to be someone else on the team who will do this. Who *can* do this."

"There is, but I want you."

"Why?" I was beyond confused.

"Because *Captivate* just released an article that got—" She stopped herself from finishing the sentence and took a calming breath. "Let's just say, it got a lot more hits than our highest-read article in history."

*Captivate* was another online magazine for women and *Afterglow*'s biggest competition. Or the biggest competition in Eve's eyes. Her college classmate was the editor for *Captivate* and Eve's main rival. From the rumors I'd heard, they had once been friends and come up with the idea for an online magazine together. At some point, they'd had a falling-out and started their own companies. I didn't know the full story or if the rumors were true, as I never felt comfortable asking.

"This year, since Hayley is out, I want to do a series on what it's like for someone who doesn't exercise to train and complete a triathlon. I even came up with a name. Track Lydia. I know *track* doesn't rhyme with *ask*, but it's close. And this way, our readers can track your progress."

I was starting to sweat, just thinking about training for a triathlon. There was a good chance I was going to die, as my body would surely give out on me the moment I tried to do something so incredibly physical.

I needed to come up with a way to get out of this.

*Maybe I should break my leg too.*

3

*Nah, not worth the lifetime of pain.* Plus, I lived on the second floor of my apartment building, and the elevator worked only about half the time.

*I've got it.*

"You know, Hayley lives in Utah. I can't do her triathlon all the way from Minneapolis." A horrible thought occurred to me. "You don't want me to move to Utah for two months, do you?"

One of the great things about working for an online magazine was, we lived all over and did everything remotely. But if I had to move to Utah to do this thing that I absolutely didn't want to do, I was going to—

Eve laughed. "They have triathlons all over the country, Lydia. I've even found the perfect one for you to do. No traveling or moving involved. I'll send you the details in your email."

*Crap.* That hadn't worked. I needed another idea.

"I already put out a column every day. I don't know how I'll have time to write two. I wouldn't want the quality of my work to suffer."

"You only have to do the triathlon article once a week."

Because we were an online-only magazine, we put a new issue out every day rather than weekly or monthly. In a sense, we ran more like a newspaper with our daily issues, but we put out magazine content to rival *Cosmopolitan* and *Marie Claire*. And because we uploaded articles every day, it kept the readers coming back for more since they didn't have to wait a month for new content. It also helped them to not forget about us between issues.

I was relieved that I would only have to do a Track

Lydia article once a week, but it didn't mean I wanted to do it.

"And it doesn't have to earn a Pulitzer," Eve continued. "It just has to get our readers interested. I know you can do this, Lydia. Our readers love your advice column. And they are going to love hearing how a real person worked hard to do an event like this. Hayley makes everything look so easy, and people struggle to connect with her sometimes. But not you. They feel like they know you. They trust you."

*Oh, great.* Now, she was complimenting me. And I was falling for it.

"Can I at least think about it?" I asked. "I need some time to—"

"I'll give you a raise, plus a bonus, for doing the extra work."

My jaw dropped open.

"I know you've been saving for a *house*." Eve trilled the last word in a little singsong voice.

"I'll do it."

*God.* I was such a sucker.

"Great." Eve beamed. "I'll send you the info for the event and a list of apps I found that will help you train for your event. Unless you want to use some of your bonus money to hire a trainer."

I sighed in defeat. "I'll use an app."

I had tried working out with a trainer in the past. They were so expensive. I would probably blow the whole bonus if I hired one.

"Whatever you prefer."

*Oh yeah, let's make it look like I actually have some power in this situation.*

"Friday will be your first article. You won't have to do much. Tell the readers about yourself in case they don't read your column, and then the next week, you'll start telling everyone about your training."

"Okay. I've got it." I held up a thumb.

"Ooh, I gotta run. See you Thursday, and don't forget to check your email."

Eve clicked off, and the Zoom meeting ended.

I closed my laptop and banged my head against my desk. Was a concussion too much to ask for?

## TWO

LYDIA

I HAD LESS than a week to figure out how I was going to get out of the mess I had agreed to participate in. But first, I needed to get out of my apartment.

A latte was calling my name.

I stepped out of my apartment just as my neighbor's door opened and his girlfriend walked out.

"Hi, Lydia," she said to me.

"Hi, Rose." I looked at the open door and sneered at my shirtless—but *too hot for his own good*—neighbor. "Broderick."

He smirked at me. "Lydia."

Broderick DeVries—or Brode*dick*, as I liked to call him in my head sometimes—and I did not get along, and I tried to avoid him at all costs. About a month after he'd moved in, our complex had hosted a Super Bowl party in the common area, and he'd told me to my face that the dip I'd brought sucked. It was the first time I had met the guy. He parked in the guest parking all the time, making it hard for actual guests to find a spot sometimes. Also, he liked to play his music loud enough for me to hear it in my apartment. Most of the time, I didn't mind, but it was still rude.

And don't even get me started on all the women who came and went from his place. My heart went out to poor Rose. As a plus-size woman myself, I felt bad for her. I loved my body and actually liked that I had curves, but not all women were as comfortable in their own skin as I was, thanks to horrible diet culture. Rose was on the heavier side and seemed like such a sweet person. Most of the other women I'd seen coming out of Broderick's apartment were thin and attractive, and it appeared as if he preferred thin women.

I guessed I didn't actually know that Rose was his girl-friend, but she was the one I saw most often. Plus, she was clearly in love with Broderick based on the way she practi-cally swooned whenever he said anything. Cheating was just another reason to avoid relationships.

At times, I wanted to tell her that her boyfriend was a liar and a cheater, but I didn't know either of them well enough. And if I told her, would I have to tell all the women? Did they all think they were dating him?

I had no idea, and I didn't want to find out. I wanted to stay as far away from that dumpster fire as I could. I had told a friend once that her fiancé was cheating on her. She had ditched me and married his unfaithful ass anyway.

Not wanting to get involved was the reason I did the next thing.

"Oh shoot. I forgot something. Bye, Rose."

I didn't want to have to walk down the hall, the stairs, and out the front door with her and pretend like everything was okay.

I unlocked my door, stepped inside for ten seconds, and then exited again.

"I know you don't like me, but you didn't have to be so rude to Rose," Broderick said.

I clapped my hand against my chest after I finished locking up. "I'm rude?"

"Yeah. Rose is nice, and it wouldn't kill you to be nice back."

I moved closer and tried to keep my eyes off his tan, muscular chest. Why an asshole like him was blessed with such a beautiful body, I didn't know. Not only was he unfaithful, but he also didn't seem to have a job. How could he when he was entertaining ladies all day? Where he got the money to pay for his apartment, I also didn't know. Our rent wasn't cheap, and he had one more bedroom than me. I had to wonder if he was one of those trust-fund babies—but obviously the black sheep of the family.

"I am nice," I said. "And I don't think you should lecture anyone on being rude when the first thing you ever said to me was, 'Your spinach and artichoke dip needs work.' "

He lifted a shoulder and stepped out of his doorway. "Sometimes, the truth hurts, baby."

"Nobody asked you."

"I was trying to save you from embarrassment before everyone in the building ate it."

"Oh yeah, because telling me my cooking needs work in front of all our neighbors wasn't embarrassing at all."

"It wasn't all our neighbors."

I rolled my eyes and inched closer. I jabbed him in the chest. "That is a lame argument. And maybe you should

9

take your own advice. Rose *is* nice, and it wouldn't kill you to come clean with her."

His brow furrowed. "Come clean with her how?"

"As if you don't know."

He laughed in disbelief. "I don't have a fucking clue as to what you're talking about."

I poked him again. "And that is why I will never like you."

He raised his hands and shook them in mock fear. "Oh no, Lydia doesn't like me." He put his face close to mine, and I couldn't help but notice how green his eyes were in contrast to his bronze skin and his dark hair and beard. "News flash: I don't care. I know everyone else around here thinks you're charming and sweet, but I know you're not."

I gritted my teeth and pursed my lips as I got closer. "I am charming and sweet."

*Man, does he always smell this good?* No wonder Rose put up with his cheating ass.

For a moment, I let myself picture what it would be like to have sex with Broderick. All those muscles and those intense eyes staring into mine as he—

"Are you okay?" he asked me as he backed away.

I squared my shoulders. "Once I get away from you, I will be perfectly fine."

He swept his arm out. "Nothing's stopping you from leaving, baby."

I went to leave but paused because I liked to have the last word. "Stop calling me baby."

He smirked again. "Now, why would I do that?"

"Because I don't like it."

His eyes looked down at my chest. "Your nipples say otherwise."

I quickly scanned my chest to see both my nipples poking out of my shirt and bra like an indicator on a Thanksgiving turkey.

"Ugh," I groaned and stomped away.

I could hear Broderick laughing all the way down the hall.

It was only after I was on the stairs that I realized I had the perfect comeback.

*At least I know how to wear a shirt.*

I hated when my retorts came to me too late.

# THREE

## BRODERICK

I TRIED NOT to let my neighbor bother me, but sometimes, she really got under my skin.

I put the free weights back on the rack a little too roughly, and I took some calming breaths before I broke something.

Lydia Karels was judgmental and acted like her shit didn't stink, but I saw the way she looked at my clients. She narrowed her blue eyes at them when she thought no one was looking. Just because she didn't like working out—I'd heard her *nope* out of another neighbor's yoga group before the question was fully asked—didn't mean she should fault others for hiring a personal trainer to get into shape themselves.

And she really had no reason to hate me so much. Sure, I'd commented on her dip at the community Super Bowl party, but I hadn't known she was the one who'd made it. And I said it needed work. I could have said it sucked. If you asked me, I was being nice.

I'd even apologized later, but she seemed to have

forgotten that. And now, I had too much pride to remind her of that fact. I'd rather have her hate me.

Too bad I couldn't stop picturing her naked.

Every time I saw her, I got hard, and I imagined pushing her to her knees, grabbing her brown hair in my fist, and filling her mouth with something besides her smart-ass comments. I was also partial to the image of bending her over and filling her pussy so full that she lost the ability to say anything other than my name.

I thought I was a glutton for punishment because it would be a cold day in hell before Lydia let me see anything more than her nipples poking out of her T-shirt.

I sprayed down my workout equipment and wiped it clean before my next client arrived.

About a year ago, some shit had gone down at my former place of employment, so I'd opened up my own personal training business. I wasn't allowed to solicit any clients from my old gym, so I knew starting from scratch would be tough in the beginning. Especially when there were some not-so-great rumors going around about me. But thankfully, word of mouth spread, and many clients followed me. Many of them were more than happy to sign up with me since they didn't have to pay a gym fee and a personal trainer fee on top of that. It was a win-win for everyone.

Soon, I was growing out of my studio apartment. Once I had been sure I could afford it, I'd moved to my new place with two bedrooms. One bedroom was for me to sleep in, and the other was my home gym. I still kept some stuff in my living room, but I no longer felt like I was drowning in workout gear.

Last winter, I had expanded to doing online classes so

that I could teach multiple people at a time. Plus, they were able to work out in the comfort of their own home. While it was pretty popular during the cold months, I had recently cut back on some of the online classes since it was now warm outside.

At ten o'clock sharp, there was a knock at my door, and I pulled on my shirt. The majority of my clients were female, and I knew it was because they liked the way I looked, but I always tried to start off with my clothes on. I often got too hot and ended up taking off my shirt. And who was I to deny my customers some eye candy?

But that was all I was. I never got sexually involved with a client. No matter what anyone said.

I answered the door to Gina, another regular, although Rose had the record for the most classes per week.

"Hi, Gina," I said.

She smiled and walked inside.

"How was your weekend?" I asked.

"Great. And yours?"

"Good."

I would never tell a client anything other than that even if I'd had the crappiest weekend. I had learned to keep my personal life private; otherwise, some clients read too much into it. I already allowed them to come into my home. I didn't need them thinking we were more than trainer and client.

Gina hung up her purse on the coat rack I kept by my door. "What's up with your neighbor?"

"Which one?" I asked since there were about fifty people in my building.

"The one who lives to the right of you. She's a woman

—mousy-brown hair, doesn't wear makeup." She winced. "A little overweight."

I frowned at Gina's description. I knew she was talking about Lydia, but it was like she'd purposely focused on all the things women saw as a negative. A lot of guys didn't care about makeup, hair dye, nail polish, or fake eyelashes. If you asked me, women dressed up for other women more than men.

"I don't know if I would say she's overweight. Not everyone has your body type, Gina. I have a client who works out with me five days a week and eats healthy, but is 'overweight' by society's standards." I used air quotes. "Many people aren't as lucky as you."

Gina looked down at her feet. "I apologize. I didn't mean to sound judgmental."

I held my hand out. "No, I'm sorry. I didn't mean to come across as lecturing. As a personal trainer, I get frustrated that people associate skinny with healthy when that is far from the truth. I've had plenty of thin clients who were unhealthy. And as I implied, I have clients who are not thin and who are healthy."

She smiled warily. "Are you going to fire me?"

I laughed. "That should be my line." I pointed to the workout room. "How about we go and get started instead?"

"Sounds good."

As we walked toward my weight machine, I asked, "Is it upper or lower body today?"

"We did upper last time."

"Lower it is. Why don't you do your squat and lunge sets while I get the machine set up for you?"

Gina started doing lunges in the bedroom. She went

down the hall to the living room and made her way back just as I finished.

"I forgot to ask, what happened with my neighbor?"

I had thought Lydia was leaving, but she must have run down to Caribou and come back. She had a cup of coffee in her hand about fifty percent of the time.

Gina rolled her eyes. "Now, I feel foolish for saying anything."

"I'm sorry about earlier. If I gave you the impression that I'm a fan of my neighbor, I'm not. We don't get along."

"That makes me feel better." She put her hands on her hips. "She's never outright impolite to me…usually. She smiles at me when we cross paths, but there is always this silent judgment in her eyes." She chuckled. "Yeah, I know. I'm a hypocrite, and I will do better." She shrugged. "But I can't seem to figure out what I did to make your neighbor not like me. Today, she actually looked at me and shook her head."

I clenched my jaw. After I'd just talked to her about being nice to one of my clients, she'd turned around and acted rude.

"I am sorry about that. I will talk to her."

Gina's eyes widened. "Oh, no, please don't do that. Then, she'll know I said something to you."

I didn't reply right away.

"Please."

I sighed. "I won't say anything." I pointed to her. "Finish up your lunges and squats."

Gina looked relieved. "Okay."

While she turned around and finished her set, I walked

over to my stereo and connected my phone. Then, I turned up the volume a little too loud.

A few minutes later, Lydia pounded on the wall, but I pretended like I couldn't hear her.

## FOUR

## LYDIA

THE SOUND of Five Finger Death Punch blared through my living room wall. That was where I worked, which was unfortunately next to Broderick's apartment, and I gritted my teeth.

The guy normally liked to listen to rock music a lot, but all week, he'd been playing it more than normal and at a much higher volume. I'd tried pounding on my wall several times, but he'd ignored me.

It usually wasn't that bad. What my jerk neighbor didn't know was that I liked rock music and I could still work through it. I had an older brother who had been loud and obnoxious at times while growing up, so one man next door wasn't going to faze me.

But today was not usual.

It was Thursday, and I was due to turn in my first article for Track Lydia tomorrow. So far, I had written one lousy sentence and had been staring at my screen for the last half hour, hoping something would come to me.

Today was one of those days that I needed silence. I

could go over and knock on Broderick's door, but I didn't want to face him. Plus, there was a good chance that a change of scenery would help me write something.

I picked up my laptop bag and slipped my computer inside. I grabbed my purse and headed to Caribou.

Inside the coffee shop, there were only a few tables available, which was slightly disappointing. Thankfully, many of the other customers were also on their laptops, so the place wasn't loud.

I ordered a latte and a pastry and found a seat toward the front that was near the window. Sometimes, people-watching inspired writing ideas.

After I pulled out my computer and connected to the store's Wi-Fi, I opened up my document again.

*You can do this, Lydia.*

I deleted the sentence I had written and started over.

Working out has never been high on my list of priorities. The most active I've ever been was in middle school while I was on the basketball team. But for me, that was just fun, and I didn't consider it exercise.

But this year, I've been tasked with doing the annual triathlon due to my coworker's injury…

I was right. I could write this article. I reread it a couple times, fixed any errors I saw, and sent it off to Eve for proofreading.

Now that I felt good because I had accomplished that piece, my mood quickly changed as I pulled up the website Eve had sent me for the triathlon, and I realized that there was no way I could go through with it.

The event had two distance options for participants. But

even the shortest option was a quarter-mile swim, twenty-two miles on a bike, and a three-mile run.

Every year in high school, I had almost collapsed after running one mile. I usually walked most of it. How was I going to do three miles, plus swim and ride a bike? And I didn't know if it needed to be said, but I hated running.

I could feel panic set in, and I knew I needed to tell my boss she'd have to find someone else. If she had to fire me, she could. There was a good chance I would die, trying to do this event, and I was choosing life over money.

"Lydia, are you okay?"

"Huh?" I looked up from where I had been staring at my computer to see Rose standing in front of me.

She smiled hesitantly. "You look a little pale. I wanted to make sure you were okay."

"I'm going to die," I blurted out.

Her eyebrows shot up, and she looked around like she wanted someone to rescue her.

"I'm not really going to die. At least…I don't think I am." I covered my eyes with my hands. "Why did I ever agree to do this?"

"Do you want to talk about it?"

I shook my head. "I just want it all to go away." I dropped my hands and dramatically stuck out my lower lip.

Rose smiled in sympathy and pulled out the chair across from me. "It sounds like you need someone to talk to. I've been told I'm a good listener."

*Oh, what the hell?*

"I'm supposed to participate in a triathlon in a couple of months. It's for my job, and there is no way I can do it. Look at me." I held up my large latte and my pastry. "Do

I look like an athlete? I literally sit on my butt and work on a computer all day." I set my stuff down. "And that is why I'm going to die, just trying to train for this awful thing." I smiled. "How's your day going? Better than mine, I hope."

"It's good. Why do you have to do a triathlon for work?"

"Long story short, I work for a magazine, and my boss wants our readers to follow me through my progress."

"Oh, wow, that sounds like a fun job."

I took a sip of my coffee. "Yeah, normally. I write a column called Ask Lydia. This triathlon is definitely outside of my usual topics."

"Why don't you ask Broderick to help you?"

I curled my lip. "I don't think so. Besides, what is some guy who doesn't have a job going to do to help me?"

Rose frowned.

My eyes widened, and I gasped. I put my hand up. "Oh my God, I'm so sorry." I winced. "Broderick and I don't get along, as I'm sure you know. I'm so used to saying whatever I want about him that I forgot about you and him. I didn't mean to insult your boyfriend."

Relationships sucked. I couldn't imagine finding out that my boyfriend was seeing other people because his neighbor couldn't keep her mouth shut.

Rose started laughing. Pretty hard too, I might add, like I had told her a good joke.

Meanwhile, I had no idea what was so funny.

When she calmed herself down enough to talk, she said, "You think Broderick and I are dating?"

"Uh…aren't you?"

*If they aren't dating, then…*

I leaned forward. "Are you two having an affair or something?"

"How do you not know anything about your neighbor?" she asked.

I shrugged. "I know enough to know I don't like him. That's all I need."

"First of all, I have a girlfriend."

"Oh." I scratched my head. "Then, why do I see you at my neighbor's all the time?"

"He's my personal trainer."

"Come again now?" There was no way I'd heard that right. Sure, I had noticed he had a nice body, but I'd figured that was because he didn't have a job, so he had nothing to do but work out.

Rose laughed. "He's my personal trainer. I work out five days a week with him. That's why you see me over there all the time."

"You work out at his apartment?"

"Yes. This way, I don't have to have a gym membership. I only have to pay for a trainer."

"Huh." I sat back in my chair and thought about all the women I'd seen coming and going from his place. "So, he's not your boyfriend, and he's not cheating on you?"

She smiled and shook her head. "No. As far as I know, he's single. He doesn't really talk about his personal life though."

"Wow." It looked like I had been wrong about him. "All this time, I thought you were his girlfriend, and he had all these women on the side." Seeing the constant stream of cheating had only cemented my single status.

She raised her eyebrows. "So, basically, you thought he was having sex all the time?"

I felt my cheeks heat. "When you say it like that, it sounds ridiculous."

"Not ridiculous. Just…"

"Improbable and unrealistic?" I offered.

Rose shrugged.

I held up a finger. "In my defense, he does have his shirt off all the time, and many of those women come out sweating and looking the worse for wear."

"I can't wait to tell Broderick."

I lunged forward and put my hand on hers. "Don't you dare." I could only guess how cocky he'd be with me if he heard what I thought about him. Or he'd be mad that I assumed he had sex all the time and didn't have a job.

*Eh.*

I didn't care if he was mad at me. I still didn't like him.

"Please don't say anything," I said again. "I can't imagine his ego needs any more inflating."

"So, are you going to ask him to help you?"

I straightened. "Hell no. I'd rather collapse from exhaustion."

There was no way I could let Broderick see how weak I was compared to him. I already knew he was fit, just from seeing him shirtless. He would laugh in my face if he trained me. He was the last person I wanted to feel embarrassed in front of.

"You could hire someone else."

I sighed. "But it's a lot of money. I'd probably have to join a gym first. And then to have someone actually train me in running, biking, and swimming? I'm sure the cost would be outrageous."

"Like I said, no gym membership needed with Broderick. Or he could even recommend someone to you. If you change your mind, you always know where to find him." She looked at her phone and stood. "I'd better get going. I have to get to work."

Rose left, and I woke up my computer.

I opened another email to Eve.

*Despite my first article being sent to you, I have changed my mind. I cannot go through with this triathlon. I understand that I won't get the bonus, and I am okay with that.*

*Thank you for understanding.*

*Lydia*

# FIVE

## LYDIA

LATER THAT AFTERNOON, I sat in front of my computer for our weekly Thursday meeting. I kept waiting for Eve to tell everyone about the project and see if there were any takers, but so far, she hadn't said anything about it. Not even after Hayley showed everyone her leg in a cast.

Earlier, I had been panicking so much about the dreadful project my boss had put on me that I completely forgot about the meeting. I was beginning to wonder if I should have waited to send my email until after, so Eve didn't ask me to talk after the meeting again.

It helped that I had an excuse today. I was due to pick up my niece and nephew from school soon. Their daycare provider that they normally went to after school was closed today, and since my brother and sister-in-law both worked outside the home, I'd offered to help.

But I could still feel my stress starting to rise as we neared the one-hour mark. Today was a day I should have laid off the coffee.

"I think that's it for today. Unless anyone else has something I missed?" my boss asked.

I wasn't sure, but I felt like she was looking right at me. But it was a camera. Everyone probably thought that.

There were some head shakes, but before Eve could call an end to the meeting, I spoke up, "I have to go now to pick up my niece and nephew." I purposely looked at my watch for emphasis. "So, if anything else is mentioned, please fill me in later."

A few coworkers said bye, but Eve said, "Lydia, I was hoping you'd have a minute to talk."

I grimaced sympathetically. "I'm sorry. If I don't go now, I won't make it to the school in time." I waved. "Good-bye, everyone."

I signed off and sat back in my chair with a sigh of relief.

I'd barely dodged that confrontation.

For now.

I was sure Eve would try to get ahold of me later, but right now, I had an elementary school to get to.

---

My phone rang in my purse at least once while I was driving, but Minnesota had a hands-free law when someone was behind the wheel, so thankfully, I had an excuse to ignore it since there was a chance it could be Eve. She didn't need to know that I hadn't hooked my phone to my Bluetooth when I'd gotten in my car.

I had a headache and didn't want to talk to her right now.

I got to the school a little early and got behind the line of cars. It gave me enough time to dig out some painkillers from my purse while I waited for the kids.

Soon, it was my turn to pull up to the front of the school, and I smiled when I saw Tabitha and Eugene running toward me. Tabitha was eight and in the third grade. Eugene was five and in kindergarten.

"Auntie Lydia," they said when I got out of my car.

"Hey, you two. How was school?" I asked as I helped Eugene get in his car seat and Tabitha buckled into her booster seat. The seats were hand-me-downs from a friend that I used for my niece and nephew, and having my own set sure made things easier, so I got to take them places.

"Good," Tabitha said.

I smiled and got back behind the wheel. We chatted about school as I drove to their house, so it wasn't until we were about halfway there that I remembered I'd forgotten something.

"Oh shit." I winced at my language. "I mean, shoot."

"Lydia sweared," Eugene helpfully informed his sister. He was still working on some of his past-tense words.

"That's right; I did. Don't tell your dad, okay?"

"What's wrong, Auntie Lydy?" Tabitha asked.

"I forgot something I need to give to your dad. Now, I will have to find another time to bring it over," I said with a sigh.

"Let's go to your place," Tabitha said.

"Yeah, let's go to your house. Let's go to your house. Let's go to your house," Eugene chanted.

I laughed. "But there is nothing exciting about my house. I mean, apartment."

Eugene always called my place a house, and sometimes, I ended up repeating him.

"We always go to our house, Auntie," Tabitha said.

It would save me time if I went to my apartment. I could always take the kids over after my brother or sister-in-law got off work. Or maybe one of them would come and pick the kids up.

I looked in the rearview mirror and made eye contact with both of them. "I guess we're going to my place."

"Yay," the kids shouted.

---

When we got to the apartment, I remembered why I didn't like taking my niece and nephew there in the first place. Really, it was just my nephew. He was the most friendly and curious person I knew. He talked to everybody we walked past, and he wanted to knock on every single door to see what their apartment looked like on the inside.

"Who lives there, Aunt Lydia? And who lives there? Do you know who lives there?"

*No, kid, I don't know. Now, stop asking.*

"Eugene, we need to go upstairs. We are not going to bug all my neighbors. Haven't you ever heard the phrase, *Curiosity killed the cat?*"

"No."

*Figures.*

We were almost to my apartment, but for some reason, Broderick's door was open, and Eugene couldn't resist looking inside.

"What's that?" my nephew asked as he pointed into my neighbor's apartment.

"Don't know." *Don't care.* "Let's go," I said as I unlocked the door and walked inside.

I held it open for both kids, but only Tabitha entered. She threw her bag on the floor, ran for my couch, and grabbed the remote.

The one thing I did have at my place that the kids liked was Netflix. Their parents were pretty strict about how much TV they watched. But I was the aunt, so I got to be more lenient.

I stuck my head out into the hall because Eugene hadn't followed his sister through the door yet. But Eugene was nowhere to be found.

I heard a, "Cool!" from Broderick's apartment.

I gritted my teeth and marched next door.

"Eugene, where are you?" I yelled as I walked inside.

The place smelled good, which I found surprising. I guessed I'd thought it would stink of old gym socks or something like that. But it didn't smell like anything of the sort.

"In here."

I headed to the bedroom where I'd heard Broderick's voice come from. It was the bedroom that shared a wall with my apartment, and it was filled with workout equipment. It seemed that Broderick really was a personal trainer, and I felt a little bad for thinking that all he did every day was mess around with women.

Of course, the personal trainer in question was only wearing shoes, socks, shorts, and a gorgeous sheen of sweat.

"Does this belong to you?" he asked, nodding toward my nephew.

29

I sighed. "Yes. I'm sorry. I told him not to come in here." I turned to my nephew. "Eugene, let's go."

"But look at all this stuff, Aunt Lydia. I want to get muscles too." He held up his little five-year-old arm.

"Not today, kid. Let's go."

"Ouch, Lydia," Broderick said.

Didn't this man understand I didn't want to be in his presence any longer than I had to?

"I'm sorry, Eugene. You can get muscles just like Broderick someday. But today is not that day. It looks like Broderick was busy before you came in here. We should let him get back to whatever he was doing." I looked up at my neighbor. "Besides, you can't just burst into other people's homes. You don't know if the person living there can be trusted."

Broderick lifted an eyebrow at my obvious jab at him.

Meanwhile, Eugene looked up at Broderick as if he were the one he needed permission from.

I gritted my teeth.

"You'd better listen to Lydia," Broderick told my nephew. "I'll help you work out and get bigger later. Someday, when you're older."

Eugene's face brightened. "Really?"

"If I'm still living next door to your aunt, I'd be glad to show you some things you could do to build muscle."

Eugene jumped up and down. "Yay."

I stepped forward and grabbed his hand. "Time to go, bud."

I looked up to tell Broderick sorry, but I didn't realize how close we were now, and for some reason, I lost my ability to speak. It wasn't fair that he was so good-looking. And I really didn't want to have dirty thoughts about him.

I yanked on Eugene's hand, and thankfully, he followed me to the bedroom door.

"Sorry about him," I said over my shoulder, not quite looking at my neighbor, and then I hurried back to my place.

Once we were inside, I shut my door and locked it, resting my head back against it. I still had my headache.

Thankfully, Eugene saw that his sister was watching a cartoon, and he ran over to the couch to sit beside her.

I grabbed my phone and headed for my recliner. I could scroll through social media while the kids watched TV. I saw that my missed calls were from my brother and not my boss at all, which was a relief. I sent my brother a quick text and told them the kids were at my place and to let me know when they wanted to pick them up.

My brother replied almost immediately.

> Eli: Since the kids are at your house, would you mind keeping them for dinner, so I can take the wife out for a nice meal?

I should have seen this coming. My brother was ever the opportunist.

> Me: Sure.

> Eli: Thank you. Please make sure the kids eat something healthy.

> Me: You got it. Just give me a heads-up before you come pick them up.

I set my phone down on the end table and asked, "Who wants pizza for dinner?"

Both kids shouted, "Me, me," and I smiled to myself.

Then, I closed my eyes and hoped my headache went away before it was time to put in our order.

## SIX

## BRODERICK

AFTER I SHOWERED AND DRESSED, I walked out of my bathroom to see Lydia's nephew standing in my living room.

"Uh, what are you doing here?" I asked him.

"You said I could lift weights."

"I did say that. But I also think I said, *someday*."

"It is someday."

The kid had me there.

"Does your aunt know you're here?"

Eugene shook his head. "No."

"Where is she?" I asked, wondering if she was going to burst into my apartment at any minute.

He shrugged. "Sleeping. She said she had a headache. But she said she was going to order pizza." He headed to my weight room. "Can I stay here?"

I didn't mind. I didn't have any more clients today. But I wasn't sure how Lydia would feel about that.

Then again, according to Eugene, she'd had a headache

and fallen asleep. I figured he was better in my care than in hers.

"Give me a minute," I told the kid. I grabbed a sticky note from a drawer in my kitchen and quickly wrote a message. I went over to Lydia's apartment and stuck it on her doorframe in hopes that she'd see it when she opened her door.

When I got back into my apartment, I clapped my hands together and asked Eugene, "Okay, kid, where do you want to start?"

---

## LYDIA

I opened my eyes to the familiar children's movie that Tabitha almost always watched when she came over.

I picked up my phone and looked at the time. An hour had passed.

*Holy crap.* I needed to get the pizza ordered.

I looked at Tabitha, who was sprawled out on the couch. "Where's your brother?"

"I don't know."

"Um, what do you mean, you don't know?"

"I don't know," she said again.

"Is he in the bathroom?"

I didn't wait for another *I don't know*. I went and checked, but the bathroom was empty. I then checked my bedroom and my bathroom in there. Also empty. There was no Eugene in my kitchen either.

My heart started racing at the realization that my nephew was missing, and I felt like I couldn't breathe.

"*Tabitha*," I barked. "When was the last time you saw your brother?"

She sighed and sat up slowly. As if there wasn't an emergency happening at the moment. "I don't know."

I rubbed my temples. If I had to hear her say that one more time, I didn't know what I was going to do. "Did he watch the movie with you? Did he leave at a certain scene?"

She seemed to think about it. "He left right away."

That did not sound good. I sprinted over, grabbed the remote off the couch, and pressed pause. The movie had been running for as long as I'd been asleep. Eugene had been gone for an hour.

"Tabitha, you said that Eugene left on his own?"

"Yeah."

"Did he say where he was going?"

"I don't know. I don't think so."

I was about ready to pull my hair out.

I spun around in circles, trying to figure out my next step.

I didn't know if I should call my brother, call the police, or look around the apartment building and try to find him myself first. Not knowing what to do was the worst feeling in the world.

I attempted to take a deep, calming breath. I needed to think about where my nephew might have gone.

He was always curious about everything, so I decided to look around the building first.

I went back to the couch and grabbed Tabitha's hands. "Do not go anywhere."

"Okay."

"Tabitha, listen to me. Stay right here. Don't go anywhere." The last thing I needed was two missing kids.

"Okay, *fine-ugh.*"

"Promise me."

"I promise. Can I watch now?"

"As long as you sit right on the couch and don't leave, you can watch whatever you want," I said as I headed to the door.

"Yay."

When I swung open the door, something fluttered to the ground. I picked up the sticky note.

*Hey, Lydia.*
*I have your nephew. If you want to see him*
*again, bring pizza.*
*Broderick*

I clutched the note to my chest and fell back against the wall in relief.

After a second, I couldn't believe I was relieved that he was with Broderick. I hadn't seen that one coming. But I wanted to know why the hell Eugene was over there after I'd told him that he couldn't go. I also wanted to know why Broderick hadn't brought him back.

I marched next door and pounded on the wood.

"Come in," a deep voice said from the other side.

I opened it to see Eugene and Broderick sitting on the couch, playing some video game. They looked like they were having fun without a care in the world.

I crossed my arms over my chest and cleared my throat.

Broderick paused the game and looked over his shoulder at me. "Hiya, neighbor."

"Hi, Aunt Lydia." Eugene waved at me with a grin spread across his face. As if he hadn't escaped while I was sleeping.

"You're in big trouble, mister," I told him.

Broderick set his controller down and stood up. He walked over to me until he was too close for my liking. My senses were all over the place. Having just woken up and then flying into an almost-immediate panic, I wasn't prepared for his big, masculine body to be so close to mine.

"Look, I told your nephew he could hang out here," he said in a low voice. "He told me that you had a headache and fell asleep. So, I thought it best you be left alone."

Some of the anger left me. Broderick was being nice. I wasn't sure if I liked it.

"You should have told me he was here. I was scared."

"I did tell you. I left you a note."

"You could have knocked on the door and told Tabitha."

Although from my earlier conversation with my niece, she probably still wouldn't have known where her brother was.

"Who is Tabitha?"

"Eugene's sister. I forgot that you hadn't met her." I held up a hand. "Next time, call or text, okay?"

His brow furrowed. "I don't have your number."

"Oh," was my only comeback. It was lame, I knew, so I poked him in the chest to keep the upper hand. "Just don't do it again."

Broderick laughed. "Whatever you say," he said in a tone that indicated the opposite.

But now was not the time to fight, so I was going to have to let it go.

I stepped around him. "Hey, Eugene. It's time to go back to my place. I'm going to order our dinner."

"Ah, man, but I'm playing a game."

"I believe I told you that if you wanted your nephew back, you had to pay the pizza ransom," Broderick said behind me—from a spot that was too close.

*Is it hot in here?*

I turned back around and raised my chin. "Fine, you can have some pizza too."

He grinned at me. "I like my pizza with all the toppings and my crust thick," he said with a wink.

I frowned. Surely, he wasn't flirting with me.

"Do you mind if Eugene stays until the food gets here?" he asked. "Then, we can finish our game."

Definitely not flirting. He just liked thick crust.

I shouldn't say yes because Eugene had disobeyed me, but I was his aunt, not his mother.

"I'll let him stay this time." I raised my voice. "But if Eugene sneaks out again without telling me where he's going, I'm going to tell his parents."

I heard my nephew groan, and Broderick tried to hide a smile behind his hand.

He nodded. "Sounds like a plan. I'll bring him over in about fifteen minutes."

With a nod, I headed to his door and then back to my place to call one of my favorite restaurants.

I ordered cheese for the kids and a supreme for Broderick and me. Thick crust on both.

## SEVEN

## BRODERICK

"I LOVE SPRING," Rose said to me.

We were walking outside today. Rose had suggested it when she arrived at my place that morning. Never one to turn down going outside, I'd agreed it was an excellent idea.

"So, I ran into your neighbor yesterday at Caribou."

I looked at Rose to see if I could get a read on where she was going with this. "Was she rude to you?"

Rose frowned. "No."

"That's good."

"Why would she be rude to me?"

I shrugged. "No reason really. She just never seems very nice to you."

Rose started laughing, and as we continued walking, her laugh got stronger.

"Okay, I am obviously missing something here."

"If I tell you something, it can't get back to Lydia, okay?"

I wanted to tell Rose that I didn't participate in gossip. I knew as well as anyone that rumors could be devastating.

But after spending time with Lydia, her nephew, and her niece last night, I was curious. Especially after she ordered the pizza I'd asked for. I'd thought for sure she would order thin crust with plain cheese just to spite me.

*Oh hell. I'm going to go along with this.*

"Okay, tell me."

Rose started laughing again. She waved her hand back and forth, as if she was trying to stop herself. "I'm sorry." She took a deep breath and seemed to calm herself down. "So, apparently, Lydia thought I was your girlfriend."

I frowned. "I guess I don't understand why that would be funny."

"Oh, that's just the beginning. Not only did she think I was your girlfriend, but she also thought you were cheating on me with all your other clients. Basically, she thought you were just having sex *all* day with multiple women."

"Whoa." I frowned. "Really?"

Rose's smile fell. "I see that you don't think it's as funny as I did. I just thought the whole thing was so ridiculous that it was funny. I'm sorry."

"No, it's fine." I could see where she was coming from. I rubbed my chin. "So, does that mean she thought I was a sex worker or something if I was having sex with all these women?"

"I don't think so. I believe she said she thought you didn't have a job."

"Oh."

Rose put her hand on my arm. "I'm sorry, Broderick. Again, I thought the whole thing was silly because I know you're not like that. I wasn't thinking that it might offend you."

"It's okay. Really," I told her, but for some reason, it wasn't. I didn't really like the fact that Lydia thought so little of me.

"The good news is, she thought you were some kind of stud who could have sex multiple times a day."

That actually made me laugh. "Well, when you put it that way…"

"Are you mad? I shouldn't have said anything."

"I'm not mad." A little perturbed but not angry. "Did she tell you why she thought that?"

"Because all your clients come out sweaty and looking the worse for wear."

"Hmm…so you're saying she thought I was good in bed?" Because a woman didn't work up a sweat if she was just lying there.

"You're not going to say anything to Lydia, are you?"

"I'm not going to tell her what you told me." But I was going to somehow give her crap for thinking that about me. I just needed to figure out how to go about it.

"There is something you can talk to her about though," Rose offered.

"What's that?"

"She has to do a triathlon for her job, and she's worried. I told her she should hire you. That's how we started talking about you in the first place."

"What did she say when you told her I was a personal trainer?"

"Besides all the *I didn't know he had a job* talk, she didn't seem too keen on it. I get the feeling she's not your biggest fan."

"Yeah, she's not."

"But maybe you could offer to help her. Offer her a discount or something."

I raised my eyebrows. "Why would I want to do that? She doesn't like me and thought I was a jobless nymphomaniac."

Rose smiled. "Because maybe she'll dislike you a little less."

"And why would that matter?"

"Because you want to sleep with her."

I stopped walking. "I think we just crossed over the trainer-client line."

Rose turned to me. "Don't worry. I won't tell anyone. Besides, you can't tell me it's not true."

I shrugged. "So what? I'm a guy, and I think with my dick. I want to sleep with almost everyone."

She gave me a look. "I've seen the way you look at her. Like you want to devour her."

"More like kill her. She drives me nuts, always assuming the worst about me."

"Right," she said skeptically.

I sighed. So, maybe I wouldn't mind fucking the constant disapproving look off her face. I would love to make her come long and hard and see how disapproving she was after that. But it wasn't like I was obsessed with her.

"It doesn't matter. There are plenty of women out there. I don't need Lydia to like me." I started walking again. "Let's keep going."

"Okay. But it would still be a nice gesture to help her out. And maybe she'll give you a shout-out in her magazine. Free advertising."

"Hmm…" Rose was onto something there. "I didn't know she worked for a magazine."

"Yeah, she writes an advice column called Ask Lydia. I looked up her column. She writes some good advice. You should check her out."

"I might just do that."

As we walked back to my apartment, an idea began to form in my mind.

# EIGHT

## LYDIA

I OPENED up my Ask Lydia email. Some days, I had dozens of emails, and other days, I only had a handful. Readers didn't email me directly. There was a contact form on the magazine website. I did try to answer all questions. There were always some that were so confusing that I just couldn't make out what the person was asking. There were also the few who asked me out on a date or for naked pictures. Those got deleted immediately.

After I did my part, Eve would choose the most interesting questions to use for my column, where there was also a comments section—that was the beauty of an online publication—to get readers engaged. It was also my job to moderate the comments and make sure there was nothing inappropriate or abusive.

The majority of the questions for me didn't end up in an issue because there was only room for so many, but they did end up on the magazine's website under an Extras section at the end of the week on Sunday. Eve waited until then in case I got sick, so she would have plenty of questions to keep my column going. It also helped bring in traffic since we didn't put a magazine out on Sundays.

Eve thought if almost all of the questions were answered, it would encourage more people to write in. And the more people who wrote in, the more reader-grabbing questions would come in. Thankfully, the one in the Extras section were not allowed to be commented on, so I didn't have to worry about going through all of them.

I opened the first email.

*Dear Lydia,*

*I need help with my neighbor.*

*You and me both*, I thought. Except, as I read the rest of the email, I realized the two of us had very different problems.

*She doesn't like me, but I can't stop thinking about having sex with her. She's actually said some bad things behind my back, which should make me like her less. But half of me wants to fuck her, and the other half wants to choke her. Or choke her while I fuck her.*

*How do I put her out of my mind?*

*Sincerely,*

*Guy Problems*

*P.S. Even though I'm sure she would never admit it, I think she wants me too. Her nipples are constantly begging me to suck them.*

. . .

I sat back in my seat and practically fanned my face. I also looked down at my chest, where my own nipples were hard. I shouldn't get turned on by a reader's email, but we all had our faults.

For a split second, I actually wondered if my neighbor was Guy Problems, but then I laughed. *No way.*

Broderick didn't want me, and I couldn't imagine he would contact a women's magazine, asking for advice. This wasn't the first guy who had emailed me, but my neighbor didn't seem the type.

I tapped the keyboard a few times before I came up with a response.

*Dear Guy Problems,*

*I am sorry to hear you are struggling and that your neighbor has spoken badly about you. I suggest that if she is the type of person who is reasonable, you should try to have a talk with her about the things you have heard. It will be hard, but try to maintain a calm tone and try not to raise your voice. But do make sure she knows that you will not tolerate being spoken about behind your back. Hopefully, once you two can sit down and clear the air, things will get better between you and your neighbor.*

*Best of luck.*

*Lydia*

I copied the email and transferred it over to the cloud drive *Afterglow* used and where I put all the questions and my answers for Eve to look over.

I considered putting the question and answer directly on the website because part of me couldn't shake the thought that it was Broderick—plus, I could see Eve jumping on this question as soon as she saw it. As with many who worked in media, Eve thought *sex sells*. I hoped that me ignoring the sex part of the reader's question would discourage my boss from putting it in the magazine.

I read the email one more time before I closed out of it.

There was no way she wasn't going to include it. Because if most women were like me, they were now thinking about sex. Hate sex, to be exact. And sometimes, hate sex was the best sex.

There was a knock at my door, and I jumped in my seat. I had really been lost in thought.

When I opened it, I did not expect to see Broderick on the other side. And of course, my slut of a brain immediately pictured Broderick fucking me.

"Are you okay?" Broderick asked. "You look a little flushed." His eyes traveled down to my chest. With a raised eyebrow, he said, "Was I interrupting something?"

A war raged inside my head. I could cover up my chest, but then I would be letting him know that it bothered me that he was looking at my nipples. Anyone else, I wouldn't have a problem, but for some reason, I didn't want this man to know it bugged me.

My other option was to pretend like I didn't care if he looked, but I feared my traitorous nipples would only get harder. Especially if he continued to look at me the way he was.

It was like he was burning a hole in my shirt. I did not

like that my body was attracted to this man.

"I'm kind of busy," I told him. "Is there something I can help you with?"

Broderick put a hand to his ear. "I don't hear any screaming, so you must have tied your victim up pretty well. Be gentle with him." He nodded toward my chest. "Those babies look like they could kill."

"You're a riot," I said drily. "And I am busy. I'm working. If my breasts could in fact kill a man, I would have taken you out long ago."

Broderick howled with laughter. My joke was not that funny, which meant he was laughing at me.

I moved to close my door, and he put up a hand to stop it from closing.

"I'm sorry."

I narrowed my eyes at him.

"I'm serious." He blinked a couple times and slowly lost the smile on his face. "I didn't come here to tease you. It's a defense mechanism."

*A defense mechanism? What the hell did he have to defend himself from when it came to me?*

"Anyway, I spoke to Rose this morning, and she told me the two of you had a talk."

With my arousal turning to embarrassment, I winced as my flush traveled from my face to my ears. They felt like they were on fire. I calmly reached up and made sure to brush my hair over them.

I should have never talked to Rose. I should have known her loyalty was to Broderick. She barely knew me.

"I didn't—" I started to say at the same time he spoke too, "She told me about your assignment for your job."

Relief slammed into me as I realized she hadn't told him that I thought he had sex all day with tons of women.

I cleared my throat. "Oh yeah, that. I'm no longer doing that."

"Oh," he said. I could have been wrong, but it looked like he was disappointed. "What happened?"

*Why does he care?*

"I emailed my boss yesterday and told her I wasn't going to do it. There has to be someone else on the team better suited for the job."

He nodded almost sadly. *Weird.* "Well, if you do end up doing the triathlon, I'd like to help."

I narrowed my eyes suspiciously. "How much do you charge?"

He smiled. "Five hundred bucks a month, but for you, I'd do it for two fifty."

I just stared at him.

"Kidding. I would do it for free."

Now, I was really suspicious. "Why? You don't even like me."

"Who says? I like you just fine." His eyes darted to my breasts and back up to my face so quickly that I wasn't sure if I'd actually seen it. "Besides, it's free advertising for me. All I ask is that you mention me a little bit and give me some free publicity."

Okay, that made sense. And it was a good idea. Not that I wanted Broderick to be the one to train me even if having him as my neighbor would make it convenient.

"Well, the point is moot since I'm no longer doing the assignment."

"Yeah." He tapped his hand against the doorframe. "If anything changes, you know where to find me."

"I do. Thanks," I forced myself to say but then regretted it when he just had to add the last word.

He grinned. "I'll let you get back to your victim. He's probably wondering when you're going to untie him. Or ravish his body. Either way, have a good day," he said and walked away.

I stepped out. "You'd better be careful, or you're going to be my victim."

He spun on his heel when he reached his apartment, still smiling like a fool. "A man can only hope." He opened his door and walked inside.

# NINE

## LYDIA

SUNDAY MORNING, I woke up in a great mood. I'd gotten to sleep in, and I hadn't heard from Eve since our meeting on Thursday. My boss was persistent when she really wanted something, so I was surprised she hadn't tried to reach out to me to get me to do the triathlon. She'd probably already found somebody new. Whoever she picked, I hoped they weren't upset at me for accepting and then declining.

Since I wasn't in any rush, I moseyed around my apartment for a while before showering and going to get my usual morning coffee.

The place was semi-busy when I got there, so I got in line and pulled out my phone. I didn't need to look at the menu to know what I wanted.

Someone came up behind me, and I felt tingles on the back of my neck. I didn't like where this was going.

I casually looked over my shoulder to see that it was Broderick standing there.

I should have known.

It seemed that my whole body was starting to become traitorous to the man behind me.

"Hey, Lydia," he said with a smile.

"Hey, Broderick."

"How's everything going?"

I eyed him suspiciously. "Fine."

"Good. I didn't hear any screaming the last two nights, so you must have let your victim go."

I rolled my eyes. "You're not as funny as you think you are."

"Yes, I am. Just not to you."

"You make me want to be single for the rest of my life."

Broderick burst out laughing. "Aw, honey, we both know that's not true," he said with a wink.

It was a good thing my phone rang at that moment because I did not have a good comeback.

I looked down at the number to see it was Eve and sighed. Maybe I hadn't gotten lucky enough to get out of the assignment.

I probably wouldn't have answered the phone, except it gave me an excuse not to talk to Broderick anymore.

"Hello?"

"Where are you?"

This was an odd question, even from my nosy boss.

"I'm getting coffee."

"At your usual place? By your apartment?"

I frowned. "Yes. Why?" I thought that maybe she had asked where I was, so she would know if I was available to talk. "Now is not a good time to talk. Can I call you back?"

"There is no need. I'll talk to you soon." And with that, my boss hung up.

I stared at my phone for a few seconds.

"What's wrong?" All joking had left Broderick's voice.

"I don't know. That was my boss, and she asked where I was, but she didn't want me to call her back. It was an odd conversation."

"Did she change her mind about the assignment?"

I shrugged. "She didn't say a single word about that."

I was next to put in my order, so I put my phone in my pocket to worry about it later.

As I waited for my drink to be made, I went to the restroom. I didn't really have to go. Again, I was just avoiding talking to my neighbor any more than I had to.

I had a lot of mixed emotions when it came to him. He aggravated me, which I hated. But then he had been super nice to my nephew, which I liked. But I hated that I liked it. And then, if I was really honest with myself, I wanted him. Which I really hated.

So, maybe my emotions weren't that complicated at all. I hated my neighbor all around. I chuckled to myself as I left the restroom.

"What's so funny?" Broderick asked.

I shook my head. "Nothing."

"Broderick?" the barista behind the counter said.

I quickly scanned the counter and didn't see any other drinks there. "Hey, you were behind me. Why did you get your drink before me?"

"Because I just got a coffee. I try to avoid putting extra sugar in my body," he said as he went and grabbed his cup.

Behind his back, I gave him a horrified look. Just another reason to hate him. *Avoids putting extra sugar into his body?* He and I could never be friends.

"Later," Broderick said with a nod and walked away.

"Later."

I stood for a few more minutes, waiting for my drink to get finished. Once I heard my name being called out, I grabbed my cup and headed to the door.

I had to swerve around a few tables, and I noticed that Broderick was sitting at the front of the coffee shop. His seat was pushed back from his table, and his legs were sprawled out as he scanned his phone, which meant I would have to step around him because he was taking up extra room. I didn't really want to talk to him again and hoped he wouldn't notice me as I was leaving.

After making sure I wouldn't trip on his long legs, I looked up to see what appeared to be my boss walking toward the glass door. I froze in place and blinked a couple times to make sure my eyes weren't playing tricks on me.

Eve lived in New York, so the fact that she was halfway across the country and coming into my coffee shop after asking where I was did not seem like a good thing.

If I knew what was good for me, I would run and hide, but I was in shock and couldn't manage to move.

Eve opened the door and entered with an air of sophistication and authority. I had only met my boss in person a couple of times, and every time, she reminded me of Meryl Streep in *The Devil Wears Prada*, except younger. To me, she screamed New York City, and she made me nervous.

She removed her sunglasses and smiled at me the way a wild animal would smile at its prey.

*I am in trouble.*

"Lydia, just the person I wanted to see."

# TEN

## LYDIA

"EVE, what are you doing here? In Minnesota?" *In my favorite coffee shop?*

"You and I need to talk, and since I was already in town, I decided to see you in person."

I tried to smile confidently, but I could feel that I wasn't quite pulling it off. "What can I help you with?"

I didn't know why I'd bothered to ask. We both knew why she was here. But what I didn't understand was why she felt it was so important to see me in person about it. Something was off.

She folded her sunglasses, and her lips were pursed as she stared at me with a stern look. "Look, Lydia, I need you to do this assignment. I am meeting with some investors and advertisers tomorrow in Minneapolis, and I plan to pitch them Track Lydia."

Now, it made sense. She wanted to get whatever investors and advertisers she was meeting to say yes by telling them about the two-month feature articles that would revolve around me, a Minneapolis resident.

There was no way she was going to let me say no now, but I really didn't like being used. If she had told me this from the beginning, I would've understood. Instead, she had tried to bribe me.

She stepped forward, and I took a step back because I didn't want to be close to her.

"I know fans love Ask Lydia, but you are replaceable, my dear."

*My dear?* She wasn't that much older than me. Maybe ten years.

Unfortunately, I really liked my job. Really, *really* liked my job. I got to work from home, I got to set my own hours, and I loved what I did. And most of the time, I got along with my boss just fine. This was the first time I had ever felt threatened. Or maybe a better word for all of this would be *blackmail*.

She took another step, and I moved back.

"I strongly urge you to reconsider turning down this assignment." Another step forward.

I stepped back again, tripped on a big shoe, and landed in Broderick's lap.

My coffee would've gone all over me if he hadn't reached up and grabbed it from my hand.

"Is this your boss?" he whispered in my ear.

I nodded, keeping my eyes on Eve.

"Want me to kick her ass?"

I had to bite my lip, so I didn't laugh, and I appreciated the joke at the moment.

"Seriously, I would tell this bitch to go fuck herself, but I also understand it's not that easy. My offer still stands for me to help you. I'll make sure you complete this triathlon, and maybe I'll even do it with you."

I turned to look at him. His words were reassuring and gave me hope because I knew I wasn't going to tell Eve no.

"Will you make sure I don't die?"

He studied my face. "Only many little deaths, but I promise you'll survive."

I didn't know what he was getting at, but now wasn't the time.

Ten minutes ago, I had said how much I hated him, and now, he was my lifeline.

*Fuck my life.*

I looked at my boss again.

"I can tell you're going to say yes," Broderick said in my ear. "But you can't let her get away with walking all over you."

He was right.

I stood up, not caring that we were now chest to chest. "I'll do it."

A satisfied smile, bordering on a smirk, slowly slid across her face. It reminded me of the Grinch.

So, before she could pat herself on the back, I added, "But I still want the raise and the bonus."

"Of course."

"And you're going to pay for my personal trainer." I moved aside, so Eve could see Broderick. "This is Broderick, and he has offered to help me, but he will not be working for free. I am not taking my extra money and paying him."

Eve pursed her lips. "Fine."

"He also gets free advertising."

She raised her brow. "You're pushing it." She looked at

my neighbor. "I'll give you two free advertising spots. But that's it. And I get to choose where they are placed."

"Works for me," he said.

Eve looked at me again. "Do we have a deal?"

The next two months were going to suck, but hopefully, my new house would be worth it.

I held out my hand. "Deal."

Eve laughed as she left, and I almost fell back onto Broderick's lap. Thankfully, I caught myself at the last second and rotated myself to land in the chair next to him.

He slid my coffee over to me, and I took a long drink.

"So…that was intense."

"Tell me about it."

"Is your boss always like that?"

"Like what?"

"A ruthless bitch."

"She is assertive and usually gets what she wants, but she's never treated me like that before."

"That's something, I guess."

"She must really want the attention of the people she's meeting with tomorrow." I put my head in my hands and sighed.

The adrenaline was starting to wear off, and I feared I wasn't going to be able to go through with my end of the bargain. And the bad thing was, now, I had dragged Broderick into it, which made me feel guilty.

I talked a lot of smack about hating him, but *hate* was such a strong word. Really, I disliked him but not enough to damage his career.

"Are you worried?" he asked me.

I looked up. "Hell yeah, I'm worried. I don't work out. At all."

"Why don't you send me the triathlon info and let me worry about the training?" He held out his hand. "Give me your phone, and we can exchange info. I'll do some research tonight, and we can get started on working out in the morning."

I pulled my phone from my jeans, unlocked it, and set it on the table.

It occurred to me that I should probably look over his shoulder to make sure he wasn't doing anything funny with my cell, but I didn't care enough. My phone dinged, letting me know I had a new message.

He gave me my phone back. "I sent you a text, so now, you have my number. If you can get me that information for the event before the day is over, that would be great."

"I'll do it when I get home."

"In order to fit you into my schedule, you'll have to start training early in the morning."

I narrowed my eyes. "How early?"

"Six thirty."

"*Six thirty?* You're out of your mind if you think I'm going to get up that early." I usually got out of bed at eight.

Broderick shrugged. "It has to be that early. My first appointment of the day is at eight, and I need to make sure I'm back home before my other client arrives."

"Back home?"

"Yeah, babe, you're not doing a regular workout. You need to train for running, biking, and swimming. All stuff that we are going to have to go outside to do."

"This is not fair."

He smiled. "It'll be fun."

I snorted. "You and I obviously have different definitions of *fun*."

His grin changed from playful to something that looked like he had a secret only he knew about. "I wouldn't be so sure about that."

"How about this? If you can wake me up in the morning, I will train with you then. If you can't wake me up, then we'll do it later in the day."

He seemed to consider this. "If I wake you up, we train. No matter what?"

I had to hold back my smile. "Yep. And I give you my permission to do whatever you need to do to wake me up." I was going to make sure to turn my ringer off and stick earplugs in my ears, so I wouldn't hear my phone ring or the door being knocked on.

"Okay." He leaned close, and his green eyes sparkled. "Looks like you got yourself another deal. But you should know, I intend to win."

"I wouldn't have it any other way," I said innocently. Because I intended to win too.

## ELEVEN

# BRODERICK

MONDAY MORNING, bright and early, I knocked on Lydia's door.

I stood with my hands on my hips, waiting patiently for her to answer.

There were always noises going on in the apartment building as people came and went, TVs blared, and kids played. But at this time of day, it was very quiet. Not just in the hall, but it was also quiet behind Lydia's door.

I lifted my fist and pounded it against the wood.

She hadn't been joking about not getting up.

I pulled my phone from the pocket of my shorts and called her. After several rings, it went to voice mail. So, I called her again. And again. And again.

"That little shit," I muttered to myself as I shook my head and chuckled.

She had probably turned her ringer off.

I considered pounding even harder on her door, but I was sure there were still neighbors sleeping, and I didn't need them coming out and getting upset with me for making noise.

*Think, Broderick. Think.*

I tried to remember if I had ever seen Lydia with any of our neighbors. Maybe one she would trust enough to give a key to in case she got locked out. But I couldn't recall seeing her with anyone in particular. Plus, I didn't want to wake anyone else up.

They would probably think I was a stalker if I told them I needed to get into someone else's apartment. And that was *if* they had a key in the first place.

A smart man would admit defeat, but I wasn't going to be accepted into Mensa, and I wasn't going to give up.

I went back into my apartment and walked out onto my balcony. There was a wall that separated mine from Lydia's, but that was it. It took me less than five minutes to climb up on my side, cross over to her side, and jump down.

When I was younger, I'd gotten locked out of my house a lot because I constantly forgot my key. Because of this, I'd learned how to jimmy the lock on the sliding glass door of my parents' house. Fortunately—or unfortunately, depending on how you looked at it—most homes had the same flimsy locking mechanism, and five minutes later, I was inside her apartment.

I closed the door and locked it back up even though it had proven to be a fruitless effort. Thankfully, we didn't live on the ground floor.

After securing the door, I paused before continuing into the apartment, feeling like a real creeper. It occurred to me that I had technically committed a felony, but Lydia had told me I could do whatever I needed to do to get her up. And no matter how much we butted heads, I didn't think she'd ever call the police on me.

Since I had already been in her apartment the other night, I knew exactly where her bedroom was. Not that it would have been a hard find because it was a one-bedroom apartment and light was filtering through all the windows.

I carefully peeked through the open door into her bedroom. She was indeed sleeping. She also had a fan blowing and a white-noise machine running.

I pulled out my phone and called her one more time. I could see her phone on her nightstand. It sat there silent as my call went to voice mail.

She had turned off her ringer.

"Lydia," I called out from the doorway in a normal voice. I wanted to wake her up, but I didn't want to scare the shit out of her.

She didn't move a muscle, so I called her name louder. She still didn't move. I tried one more time but to no avail.

I wanted to avoid going in her room because it was her personal space, but I was beginning to think it was unavoidable.

The first thing I did was turn off her white-noise machine and her fan. Hopefully, the lack of air and noise would rouse her. But I noticed green sticking out of her ear. She had earplugs in.

I had to smile. It was no wonder she hadn't heard me knock or call her name.

It also made me feel a little less guilty about breaking into her place. She'd obviously underestimated my tenacity.

I walked over to her bed and plucked the earplugs out, figuring that would be enough to wake her up.

I laughed when she didn't move.

Cautiously, in case a fist came flying at me or my junk, I bent over and said, "This is your wake-up call," directly in her ear.

She shot up as I swerved out of the way before her head collided with my face.

"What the hell are you doing?" she yelled at me as she gasped for breath. "How did you get in here?"

"Waking you up," I said with a grin. "And I came in through the sliding glass door. You might want to invest in a sturdier lock."

"You scared the hell out of me."

"You told me to wake you up in any way I could."

She didn't look impressed with my skills. "I suppose I did."

Her chest was still heaving, and I noticed her covers had fallen off of her.

*Holy shit.*

I'd already had fantasies about her breasts. But at that moment, I knew my hand had a date with my cock later, where I was going to think about nothing but the thin white T-shirt covering the most perfect set of tits I had ever seen in my life. It was one thing to see her nipples poke out of her shirt. It was another to see the deep berry color of them.

"Get up and get dressed," I said a little too sternly. "It's time to work out."

She frowned at me. "Jeez. Crabby much?"

"Not crabby, just in a hurry. I already wasted twenty minutes getting you out of bed. We're going to have to cut your workout short today." I headed for the living room. "I'll wait outside for you."

When I got to her front door, I adjusted my dick before walking out into the hall.

It was a good thing, too, because one of our neighbors came out of her apartment the same time I came out of Lydia's, and she smirked.

So, now, the neighbor thought we were sleeping together. Lydia was going to love that.

# TWELVE

## LYDIA

"OH MY GOD, I need to stop." I put my hands on my knees as I hunched over and took big, gulping breaths. "I can't keep running like this."

Broderick had stopped ahead of me, so he backtracked to where I could see his feet in my line of sight. "We haven't even been running for five minutes."

I stood up. "That's four minutes too long. I told you, I don't work out at all."

"Why not? Let's at least walk while you tell me."

"Fine." I could handle walking and actually didn't mind it as a form of exercise. If I was forced to work out, that was. "I just don't like it." I shrugged. "I don't get that high that other people talk about, nor do I get more energy when I work out. I know it's good for me, but there always seems to be something I need to do, and I run out of time."

"When you're starting a new routine, no matter what the routine is, you have to carve out time in your schedule until it becomes a habit."

"I know that. It's not like I've never worked out in my life. Like I said, it doesn't do anything for me."

"You're wrong about that, but what you're looking for is the instant gratification. It's good for your overall health, but you can't tell, so you feel like you're not getting anything out of it."

I smiled. "Exactly. You get it."

"Not really. I like working out. That's how I relieve stress. It feels good to me. But I do get where you're coming from. You wouldn't be the first client I had who felt the same way."

"So, what is your suggestion?" I asked.

"Because you need to feel that instant gratification, you're going to have to give yourself an outside reward. Also, you need to make working out feel less like a chore."

"That's going to be pretty hard to do when I am literally doing this for money."

A soft smile spread across his lips. "This is true, but you and I will think of something. You like coffee, right?"

"I think everybody in the building knows I like coffee," I joked.

"So, maybe you don't get your morning coffee until you finish your workout. That could be your outside reward, and maybe it will encourage you to finish."

I wrinkled my nose. I really didn't want to connect the exercise and the assignment with my favorite beverage. "I'd rather get laid. Or have a spectacular orgasm as a reward."

Broderick almost tripped, and I chuckled.

"Sorry. TMI. That's what you get when I haven't fully woken up or had any caffeine."

Or that was what he got for waking me, pulling me from

an amazing sex dream. The nameless and faceless man in my dream had just been about to go down on me before I was woken up. I should probably be grateful to Broderick because I would've woken up frustrated and horny. Still, it wasn't a bad reward for completing my training for the day. Too bad I didn't have anyone to give me my prize.

"How about we just keep brainstorming?" Broderick asked.

"Yeah, that's probably for the best."

"Since you obviously hate running, we'll do little sprints in between walking. How does that sound?"

"Awful."

Broderick shot me a look.

"Okay, okay. Let's give it a try."

"I'll time us. We'll do short sprints, and every day, we can add a little time."

That sounded horrible, but it needed to be done.

"When do we get to move on to biking?"

When I was a kid, I'd loved biking and done it for fun. Even though I hadn't been on a bike for quite some time, I knew I would like it ten times more than running.

"We'll get there. One step at a time. We also have to add swimming. We'll break up your workouts, so they don't get too monotonous."

"Are we just going to swim in our building's pool? Because there are always people there."

It was nice that we didn't have to find a place with a pool, but I didn't know how I was going to actually swim laps when I would probably run into people in the water.

"We'll start out slow there too. I'm not going to worry about that right at the moment. What I am going to worry about is you completing the next two minutes of running. Are you ready?"

"I guess."

He pushed a button on his watch, I heard it beep, and he said, "Go."

---

I didn't know how much later it was because it felt like a week had passed when we were finally done with our sprints. Unfortunately, we still had a couple of blocks to go before we got back to our apartment building, and I was dragging ass.

"That's it. You're going to have to…carry me…the rest of the way back." I could barely talk; I was breathing so hard. "On second thought, just leave me here."

Broderick laughed and grabbed my arm to put over his shoulder.

"What are you doing?"

It wasn't the most comfortable way to walk, seeing as how he was several inches taller than me.

"How tall are you?"

"Six feet. And you?"

"Five-six."

We continued walking, and my breathing finally evened out from the exercise. But now, I was struggling to get in air, thanks to the feel of my neighbor so close to me.

I didn't understand how somebody so sweaty could smell and feel so good.

Which reminded me that for how sweaty he was, I was a

hundred times worse, and I pulled away. "I think I'm okay now." I smiled. "Thanks for helping me get home."

"No problem."

We reached our building, and he opened the front door for me. We slowly went up the stairs. My leg muscles were already getting sore.

"You have to work today?" Broderick asked.

"Yes."

"How often does a new magazine come out? Once a month?"

"We're an online magazine, so we actually don't have physical copies. And we put out new content every day, except Sunday."

"Wow."

"Our format is not the same as the magazine you pick up at the grocery store. We don't release a whole magazine every single day. We break it up so that readers have something new every morning, but it's not so overwhelming that they don't have time to read it. Some things are new on a daily basis, like my Ask Lydia content because only two questions are usually answered. But something like the Fitness and Fashion sections come out once a week, and they are not posted on the same day."

"That makes sense."

He made it to the top floor, and I was about to walk past Broderick's door when he grabbed my hand and pulled me back to him. "Whoa, whoa, whoa. Where are you going?"

I pointed behind me. "I was about to go take a shower."

He unlocked the door and pushed it open. "You need to stretch first, or you are going to be very sore tomorrow, and then we'll have to wait at least a day to train again."

I grinned. "Sounds great to me."

He just looked at me like I was an annoying child. "Get inside."

"I want you to know, I strongly oppose this," I said as I marched past him into his apartment.

"Noted." He pulled something from the corner of his living room. It was a rolled-up mat, which he laid out.

"I think you should also know that I don't have any more energy, so whatever you show me, I'm going to half-ass."

He smiled. "Lie down. I will help you stretch. You just have to lie there."

"Oh, thank God." I collapsed onto the mat and closed my eyes. "Wake me up when you're done."

"Is that what you say to all the guys you date?" he joked.

I opened one eye to peek at him. "I thought I tied them up? Doesn't that mean I do all the work?"

He grinned. "Oh, that's right."

I closed my eyes again as he started bending and twisting my body. There were a few times I winced, but overall, he handled me with care.

"I'm going to stretch your hamstrings now, and we'll be done."

*Whatever.* "Okay."

He bent my knee and pushed it back toward my head. Then, he slipped my leg over his shoulder, and again, he pushed it toward me.

But this didn't feel the same.

My eyes flew open as Broderick's leg rubbed against my *only covered in a thin layer* vagina. When I'd said I wanted an orgasm after my workout, I had been joking.

"Oh God, not now," I whimpered in a low voice to myself.

As he pushed on my leg, his thigh rubbed my now-swollen clit.

He frowned, oblivious to my sudden arousal. "Your muscles are tightening up. You need to relax, Lydia."

"No, I need—" *You to get off me*, was what I had been trying to say, but I didn't get to finish as my body stiffened, my back arched, and I climaxed right there on Broderick's living room floor.

He froze and slowly loosened his hold.

I couldn't move either, but my stillness was out of embarrassment, and I assumed his was shock.

I couldn't look him in the eyes.

His throat bobbed as he swallowed. "Did you just...come?"

I pushed him away with my leg, scrambled up off the floor, and ran out his door.

# THIRTEEN

## BRODERICK

I KNOCKED SOFTLY on Lydia's door.

"Lydia, open up, please."

Silence was all I got in return.

"Let me in. We can talk about what just happened."

"No." Her voice sounded far away, but at least she was speaking to me.

I dropped my forehead to her door, trying to find the right words to let her know that what had happened in my apartment was okay without actually saying the exact words out loud through her door. It wasn't easy to do, and I didn't exactly have a lot of experience with clients orgasming during post-workout.

To say I had been stunned would be pretty accurate. To say I was worried would also be accurate. But to say I was now horny as hell would be an understatement.

I supposed that I had technically been the one to make her come with the stretching, but now, I wanted to pull off her pants and put my mouth between her legs and make her do it again. On purpose this time.

"I need to make sure you stretch your other leg, so you're not in pain later."

"Ha. If you think I'm getting near you again, you're nuts. I've had enough embarrassment for one day, thank you very much." Her voice was closer now.

I couldn't stop the smile from spreading across my face. So, she was afraid it would happen again.

*Hmm…*

"You don't have to be embarrassed. Everyone does it."

"Everyone has an orgasm when you stretch their muscles?"

I laughed. "No, I simply meant that everyone has orgasms in general."

"So, I *am* the only one this has happened to with you. You just proved I should be mortified."

I sighed. "Will you at least make sure that you stretch yourself? If you don't know what to do, do a search on YouTube, Google, whatever for *hamstring stretches*. Please."

"Okay, fine."

She sounded like she was right on the other side of the door now, and I wanted so badly to come up with the right words to make her feel better.

"Would it help if I told you that I think you're sexy as hell and you have nothing to be embarrassed about? In fact, the opposite. I have to either go back and take a cold shower or spend some alone time with my hand."

I heard a soft chuckle. "You're just trying to make me feel better."

"Ha." *If only.* "I'll leave you alone the rest of the day, but I'm not letting you quit on me already. Tomorrow is a new day, and we can start over again. How does that sound?"

"I'll think about it."

It wasn't an agreement, but I would take it for now. "Okay, I'll leave you alone then. We can talk later."

"Thank you."

"As long as you promise to finish stretching," I added.

"I will."

I headed back home and paced for a few minutes before Holly showed up. I wasn't much in the mood to talk, and she didn't seem to mind. After she left, I knew I had to get some perspective.

"Hello?"

"Hey, Travis," I said into my phone.

Travis was an old friend. Years ago, we'd worked together and stayed friends after he went to a gym closer to where he lived and I moved to a gym that would end up being my downfall.

"Hey, man."

"Do you have a minute?"

"Uh…yes, I have a few. What's up? You sound serious."

"Have you ever had a woman come while you were training her?"

"Oh…wow…uh…"

"Your wife doesn't count, dude."

Travis chuckled. "Then, no. Although I don't think I've ever technically trained Sydney. More like worked out alongside her. But that's not important. I want to hear more about why you asked the question."

"I'm training my neighbor right now."

"Which one?"

"The one with the breasts." I sounded like an ass, but I might have told my friend about her great boobs.

Travis laughed. "The one you don't like?"

"I never said I didn't like her."

"Sure you did. After you told me she didn't like you."

"Maybe."

"So, I take it, you don't hate her anymore if you're handing out orgasms to your clients."

I knew he was trying to lighten the mood with a joke, but I was worried.

"It's more complicated than that. I am helping her train for a triathlon that she has to complete for her job." I explained to him about Lydia's assignment and how I was getting some good PR out of the situation. "Anyway, today was the first day. I was helping her stretch after we went for a run since her body isn't used to physical activity, and I guess my leg was hitting just the right—or wrong—spot because she froze up on me and then…exploded."

"Holy shit."

"You're telling me."

"What happened after that?"

"She got up and ran to her apartment. I tried to talk to her, but she wouldn't come out."

"Yeah, I bet."

"I told her I'd give her time, but I don't want her to find someone else to train her. I need the exposure. Not only will she mention me in her articles, but the free ad space I'll also get will be great. It can get my name out there to people outside of Minnesota. I really want to work more on my live online classes."

"I thought things were going well with your business? You just moved into a bigger place not that long ago."

"Things are going well, but what happens when they

aren't? I'm doing okay, but I'd like a little security. I had to sacrifice a lot of my savings after everything went downhill at the gym."

"Look, Broderick, you are your own boss now. There's no manager breathing down your neck or some corporate office states away that doesn't care who you are. And I highly doubt that your neighbor is going to go telling everyone that she had an orgasm."

"Oh…shit. I didn't even think of that."

"Hey, that's a good sign. Maybe you aren't as cynical as I thought you were."

I chuckled. "Yeah, well, she was pretty embarrassed, even when I told her she didn't have to be. I'm pretty sure she won't tell anyone." I waved my hand back and forth even though Travis couldn't see me. "We're kind of getting off track. I called to see what I should do, but it seems like I'm the only one who's been in this situation."

"I'm no expert in women even though I'm married to one, but I would give her the rest of the day to let the embarrassment fade a little. Talk to her tomorrow and maybe just play it cool, like nothing happened."

"I did mention starting things over between us."

"There you go. Unless things are weird between you two, don't bring it up. And for God's sake, try to forget about what happened."

"You're assuming I want to remember."

"I've known you a long time. I'm not assuming anything. I know you probably liked it."

He had a point. Even worried, I couldn't stop picturing what Lydia had looked like, coming underneath me.

"How would you feel if that happened with you and Sydney?"

"I'd take off our clothes and make love to my wife."

"Forget I asked."

Travis laughed. "Seriously, Broderick. The situation in your past is unlikely to happen again, and you're not going to fire yourself. But this woman does work for a magazine. Don't do anything to piss her off, so she writes a tell-all about you."

I frowned. "I don't think she'd do that."

"I hope you're right. But then again, I know that you'll handle the rest of her training with professionalism."

"Damn right I will. And I'm going to make sure she does a good job in two months too."

"Good." I heard some sounds, as Travis must have been moving around. "Speaking of clients, my next one should be here soon, so I'd better go."

"Okay."

"Let's have dinner with everyone later this week."

"Sounds good."

"I'll send out a text after work."

"Okay. Later."

"Later."

I hadn't really resolved anything, speaking with Travis, but I did feel better. I didn't know Lydia that well, but she was a good person.

And speaking of Lydia...

Since I'd told her I would give her space, I turned on my laptop and went to her magazine's website. I went to the Ask Lydia section to see if my question had been posted. I doubted it would make it, so when I saw my handle, Guy Problems, I was shocked.

I quickly reread my question before moving on to her answer.

It left me a little disappointed. Her advice was solid, but she didn't mention anything about how I wanted to have sex with her.

I clicked on the contact form and began to type.

# FOURTEEN

## LYDIA

AFTER BRODERICK LEFT MY DOOR, I followed his instructions and finished stretching, mostly because I didn't want to be sore tomorrow. But also because I didn't want him to help me again.

I also showered, hoping that could wash away my humiliation.

It didn't work.

I guessed it was a good thing that I had work to do. I pulled up my email and opened the oldest email first. I began to write responses to the readers' questions. Reading some of the things that people went through made my problem seem like not as big of a deal.

So what if I'd had an orgasm in front of my neighbor? At least my boyfriend wasn't cheating on me, a good friend hadn't ghosted me, or my mother wasn't trying to control my life.

The worst was a high school girl whose boyfriend had hit her. I told her to get out right away, and I could only pray she listened to my advice. I hoped Eve posted this question in the magazine. I could see many women commenting, telling their own thoughts and experiences, encouraging the reader even more to get out of her relationship.

I was almost to the end when I saw the name Guy Problems at the bottom of the email. He had emailed me again.

*Dear Lydia,*

*I saw your answer to my question, and I appreciate your advice. I have not approached my neighbor yet to talk with her, but I will do so soon.*

*However, I am writing to you today because you didn't tell me how I could stop thinking about her sexually.*

*I recently saw her in a more intimate setting—it's a long story —and now, I'm thinking about her even more.*

*Please help.*

*Sincerely,*

*Guy Problems*

Alarm bells went off in my head again as I pictured Broderick writing this.

But there was no way. *Right?*

I shook off my worry. I hadn't even looked to see if Eve had posted the question in an article or in the Extras section on the website.

I quickly pulled up *Afterglow* on my computer and went looking. It wasn't in the Saturday edition, but today was a different story.

Right under my first article for Track Lydia was Guy Problems's question. Eve had put my new assignment in between the Fitness section and my advice column. I had to hand it to her. She was smart when it came to marketing. Fitness readers might read Track Lydia and go on to read Ask Lydia. And Ask Lydia fans might scroll back up to read Track Lydia.

And—*holy shit*—there were already hundreds of comments under the question from Guy Problems. It had only been posted this morning. I couldn't believe how many responses there were. It was going to take me forever to go through them all.

ANONYMOUS WROTE:

SCREW YOUR NEIGHBOR. YOU CAN COME OVER TO MY PLACE ANYTIME. I WON'T SPEAK BADLY ABOUT YOU.

ANONYMOUS WROTE:

*FANS FACE* WOW. YOUR NEIGHBOR DOESN'T KNOW WHAT SHE'S MISSING.

DINA WROTE:

I ONCE HAD A NEIGHBOR WHO TALKED BEHIND MY BACK ALL THE TIME. THE BEST THING I EVER DID WAS MOVE OUT OF THAT BUILDING. BEST OF LUCK TO YOU, GUY PROBLEMS.

ANONYMOUS WROTE:

YOU CAN CHOKE ME OUT ANYTIME, GUY PROBLEMS. AND SUCK ON MY NIPPLES.

. . .

There were a lot of sexually explicit comments on the thread and most of them posted by people who didn't want to give their names. Commenters like Dina were rare.

I didn't really understand it. They didn't even know what the guy looked like. They'd just assumed by one email that he was hot. I wished I could ask these women why.

And all these responses made my job of answering his next question even harder. I considered deleting the email and not answering because there was no way that Eve wasn't going to put it in the next article after the response the magazine had gotten to the first question.

However, I would never underestimate my boss again. This was a company email, and who knew what she kept track of? Especially since she'd blackmailed/bribed me to do the fitness assignment. She might be keeping an extra-close eye on me because of that.

I was screwed.

I finished going through the comments and only had to delete a couple. One was spam, asking people if they wanted to make money from home. Another was from a woman who had given her phone number. The magazine didn't need the woman getting harassing phone calls and then have her blame us for the abuse.

Surprisingly though, there were no comments from Guy Problems. Although he probably thought that nobody read the comments, which was why he had emailed me again.

Since I wasn't going to be able to avoid the sex part of his question again, I needed to word my answer carefully.

I sat back in my chair and started brainstorming.

I was so lost in thought that I jumped when music began to blare from Broderick's apartment.

The song?

"I Touch Myself" by Divinyls.

I wanted to be mad, but I couldn't help laughing, so I picked up my phone.

> Me: You'd better be careful, or whatever client you're with is going to think you're talking about them.

I set my phone down, not expecting a response until he was finished with his client session.

It wasn't until the next song, the less blatant "Blister in the Sun" by Violent Femmes, that he answered.

> Broderick: I'm all alone. I thought that was obvious.

I laughed.

> Me: So, you're over there, masturbating?

> Broderick: Wouldn't you like to know?

> Me: You're right. I don't want to know.

> Broderick: Do you want me to send you a video, so we're even?

> Me: Even?

> Broderick: Yeah. I saw you come. And this way, you can see me come. We'll be even.

I bit my lip. I would way rather see that in person.
I did not tell him that though.

> Me: I thought we were starting over. We're supposed to not talk about it and forget this morning ever happened.

Broderick: We can start over, and I can promise not to bring it up. But I'm sorry, babe. There is no way I'm ever forgetting this morning. I do promise not to bring it up, if that helps.

> Me: How am I supposed to face you tomorrow if you won't forget?

Broderick: That's why I offered to show you, so we're even.

> Me: What advice would you give to someone who confided in you that they wanted to have sex with someone they don't like?

Broderick: Is that an invitation?

> Me: No. Just give me an answer.

Broderick: LOL. I would tell them they needed to fuck the person to get them out of their system.

> Me: Thanks. Gotta go.

Broderick: Wait.

Me: What?

Broderick: Why did you ask?

Me: It's for work.

Broderick: You're actually going to print what I just wrote?

Me: No. I asked what you would do, so I could tell the reader to do the opposite.

Broderick: If I didn't like you so much, I'd come over there and choke you for being so mean to me.

My eyes widened at his use of the word *choke*. *Does he read the magazine? No.* I refused to believe it.

I put my phone on silent and turned it upside down without answering.

I was such a chicken.

## FIFTEEN

# BRODERICK

THURSDAY EVENING, I went to meet my friends for dinner at one of our favorite restaurants. Dan and Lilah were already at the restaurant when I arrived, and Travis and Sydney came in about a minute after me.

"No date tonight, Broderick?" Lilah asked.

"Nah."

"You haven't brought someone to dinner for about two months now," Travis said.

I shrugged. "No one worth bringing, I guess." A vision of Lydia flashed in my mind.

"Maybe they're just all sick of you."

I gave Dan the finger.

"They're so mean to you," Sydney said. "Leave Broderick alone," she told the group.

Travis put his arm around his wife. "Broderick is a big boy. And he's been bringing various women to our dinners for years." He leaned close to me. "Does this have to do with a particular neighbor?"

I shook my head. "No. I've been busy, and I haven't had much time to date."

Lilah put her hand on her chest. "I think our little boy is growing up."

"Maybe I secretly want you," I said. "And since I can't have you, no one else will do."

She snorted. "Yeah, right."

"You're right." I smiled coyly at Dan. "It's your husband I really have the crush on."

"You snooze, you lose, bro. I'm married now."

I snapped my fingers in mock disappointment. "Damn."

Our server came over then, gave us our menus, and took our drink order. As she walked away, movement caught my eye, and I looked over to see someone approach the bar right by our table.

"Lydia," I said.

She turned, and surprise lit her face when she saw me. "Broderick. Hi."

Things had gone well the rest of the week. I hadn't brought up what had happened between us on Monday, and she hadn't tried to avoid me. In fact, every morning, she was waiting outside my door to train.

She was slowly improving too. She had a ways to go, but I was confident she'd be able to complete her triathlon when the time came. She wouldn't get the best score, but she'd make it through.

"Broderick, introduce us," Lilah said.

"Oh. Sorry." I smiled. "This is my neighbor, Lydia. Lydia, these are my friends—Lilah and Dan, and Travis and Sydney."

She held up her hand in a wave. "Hello."

"Are you picking up food?" Lilah asked.

"I plan to. It was a last-minute stop, so I didn't call in an order."

The bartender walked up at that moment. "Did I hear that you'd like to put in an order?"

"Why don't you eat with us?" Travis said.

I swung my head around to look at him, but he was looking at Lydia.

"Yeah, you should join us," Lilah said.

Lydia swallowed and licked her lips, as if she was unsure what to do.

Travis kicked me.

I looked at him again, and he jerked his head toward Lydia.

*Oh. Right.*

"Lydia, you're more than welcome to join us," I told her.

She seemed to think it over and turned to the bartender. "I think I'll eat with them."

"I'll have someone bring you a menu. Can I get you anything to drink?"

"Water, please."

We were sitting around a booth, where I was in the middle, so I wasn't expecting Sydney and Travis to start sliding to get out.

"We'll move, so you can sit by Broderick," Travis told her.

"That's okay. I can sit on the end," she said.

"It's no big deal," Sydney said.

A few seconds later, Lydia was sitting next to me.

"So, what do you do, Lydia?" Lilah asked.

"I work for an online magazine called *Afterglow*."

"I read that." Lilah gasped. "Wait. Are you Lydia from Ask Lydia?"

Lydia blushed. "I am."

"I love your column. When I was little, I used to read Ann Landers. Advice columns are the best."

"I used to read Ann Landers too. And I even read it when the column changed to Annie's Mailbox."

"Sydney's a writer too," Lilah pointed to Travis's wife.

Sydney waved her hands back and forth. "I write romance novels. I could never give anyone advice."

Lydia laughed. "Well, I think it's cool that you write novels. I tried once, and I just couldn't do it. Shorter things are much easier for me to write."

"Oh my God," Lilah said.

We all turned back her way.

"What?" I asked.

She held up her phone. "There's this guy who has written to you a couple times it looks like. And he is gaining some fans."

I tried to show no emotion because I knew she was talking about me. When I'd sent my questions in, I hadn't meant for all these women to want me. They didn't even know who I was.

"Oh, I know. I've had to delete several phone numbers from the comments," Lydia said.

"What does it say?" Travis said.

Lilah read off my first question and Lydia's response. Then, she continued, "And here's the second question: *Dear Lydia. I saw your answer to my question, and I appreciate your advice. I have not approached my neighbor yet to talk with her, but I will do so soon. However, I am writing to you today because you didn't tell me how I could stop thinking about her sexually. I recently saw her in a more intimate setting—it's a long story—and now, I'm thinking about her even more. Please help. Sincerely, Guy Problems.*"

Lilah took a deep breath. "*Dear Guy Problems. Please forgive me for neglecting this part of your question from your previous email. Unfortunately, being attracted to someone is a feeling, and we cannot control how we feel. We can only control how we act on those feelings. I suggest that you ask someone else out on a date. Perhaps the start of a new relationship will help you move past your feelings for your neighbor. However, since you have not spoken to your neighbor yet, maybe things will improve between you two, and a truce can be called. If that happens and your neighbor is attracted to you, as you suspect, perhaps you can ask her on a date. Whatever you decide to do, please don't force anything. These feelings won't stick around forever. It might just take longer than you'd like. Sincerely, Lydia.*"

Lilah put her phone down.

"Wow," she said. "That was so well put. I would have had no idea what to say back to someone who asked such a loaded question."

"Thank you," Lydia said. "I asked Broderick what his advice would be, and I simply went in the opposite direction."

Travis laughed. "And what was his advice?"

"That Guy Problems should fuck his neighbor out of his system."

"*Broderick,*" Lilah said.

I shrugged. "It sounds like solid advice to me."

"But only if the other person is willing," Lydia said.

I looked at her. "Oh, she's willing all right."

Lydia's brow furrowed in confusion, and then her eyes opened wide.

"How would you know?" Dan asked.

*Shit.*

I looked away from Lydia. "I don't. Guy Problems said she was, so I'm just assuming."

"Hmm…" she said. "He said that in his first email to me. Not this last one. Is someone reading my magazine?" she asked, her tone teasing.

I shrugged. There was no good answer to her question.

"Well, if his neighbor isn't up for anything, there are plenty of women in the comments who are," Lilah pointed out.

"Yeah, too bad they don't have a way of finding each other," Lydia said.

"Maybe you should stop deleting their phone numbers," I joked.

She gave me a deadpan look. "That's for their own safety. I doubt Guy Problems would call any of those women. But someone else probably would. And then *Afterglow* would have a lawsuit on its hands."

I nudged her with my shoulder. "I was teasing you. You need to lighten up."

She smiled warily. "Sorry."

It was at that time that our server came back to take our orders, and all talk of Guy Problems—aka me—was done.

## SIXTEEN

## LYDIA

DINNER WITH BRODERICK and his friends was fun. It was better than getting takeout and eating at home while I stared at my computer, figuring out what I was going to write for my Track Lydia article. I would have to worry about that tomorrow.

"We'd better call it a night," Lilah said. "Gotta get up for work early in the morning."

Sydney yawned. "Yes, bed sounds wonderful right now."

We had already paid our bills, so with nothing keeping us there, we all stood up and filed out of the restaurant.

"It was nice meeting you, Lydia. You should come out with us again sometime," Sydney said.

"I agree," Lilah said.

"It was nice meeting all of you too. And I think I'd like that," I told them.

I exchanged phone numbers with the two of them, and then we all started walking toward the parking lot, except for Broderick.

"Aren't you coming?" I asked him.

He smiled. "I walked here."

"But it's, like, two miles away."

He laughed. "I know."

I would never get used to how active he liked to be.

I noticed that everyone had gone, and it was just the two of us. The sun was going down, and by the time he got home, it would be dark. I wouldn't want to walk home alone at night. Although I wasn't a muscular, fit man, so Broderick probably didn't mind.

"Do you want a ride?" I asked. "I know how much you like your exercise, but it'll be dark soon."

"Sure. I'd rather save my energy."

"Then, why did you walk here?" I asked as we went to my car.

"Plans changed."

"Oh. Can I ask what you need this extra energy for?"

"You'll see."

We reached my car, but I didn't unlock it. "If you're going to make me do some sort of workout when we get home, the answer is no. We already worked out this morning, and I have to do it again tomorrow. I refuse to do anything more."

He laughed. "Just get in the car, Lydia. I'm not going to make you do anything you don't want to do."

I studied him, but I couldn't tell if he had something up his sleeve or not. In the end, we couldn't stand in the parking lot all night, so I unlocked my car and got behind the wheel.

Walking two miles would have taken some time, but driving that short distance got us back to our building rather quickly. I drove past the parking lot to the underground garage and noticed Broderick's car, which was where it was supposed to be tonight.

"Why do you park in guest parking? It's not fair to the guests."

He turned and looked before we went down into the garage. "It's farther away from the building. I like to walk."

"Yeah, I know."

He chuckled. "And that way, guests can park closer to the building."

And here I'd thought, he did it because he didn't care about others.

"I can see you're trying to be nice, but guests don't know that there is an open spot in the tenants parking. Not unless they're your guest. You're actually just making one less spot for guests and therefore making it harder for them to find a spot."

"Hmm, I suppose you're right."

"Wow. I didn't think you'd agree with me," I said as I pulled into my reserved parking space.

Broderick laughed as we got out of the car. "Why wouldn't I agree with you? When you're right, you're right. It's not that big of a deal."

"I guess I thought you didn't like me."

I didn't know why I was being so open and honest with him. It wasn't like I'd had any alcohol with dinner.

"I like you just fine. You're the one who doesn't like me."

"Well, you do play your music really loud, and you did tell me that my food sucked at the Super Bowl party."

He held up a finger. "I believe I said it needed some work." He bumped his shoulder into me. "And in my defense, I didn't know it was your dip."

I shook my head with a laugh. "I don't know if that makes it any better."

"Would it help if I said I was sorry?"

"Maybe," I teased.

We reached his door, and I watched him unlock it. I wasn't quite sure what I was waiting for that I didn't continue down to mine. A good-bye? Something more?

Broderick pushed the door open and leaned against the jamb. He smiled. "Is there something I can do to make it up to you?"

"I don't know. I mean, you are already training me."

"What about if I licked your pussy and made you come again?"

I gasped.

He grabbed my hand and pulled me inside his apartment.

The sun had set, and the lights were off, but the shades were open, and the moon and streetlights gave off plenty of illumination.

As he kicked the door shut and pushed me against the wall, he asked, "Riddle me this, Lydia. Am I your trainer who happens to be your neighbor? Or am I your neighbor who happens to be training you?"

It was kind of an odd question, but his face was serious, so I understood that this was important to him.

"Neither."

His brow rose. "Oh?"

"I'm your friend who you are doing a favor for."

He licked his bottom lip and smiled. "What if I want to be more than friends?"

"How so?" My question came out as scarcely more than a whisper, and I realized it was hard for me to breathe.

He kissed my neck. "As much as I like Travis and Dan, I don't want to lick their pussies."

I leaned my head back until it hit the wall and met his eyes. "What about Lilah and Sydney?"

"I don't want to lick their pussies either. Just yours." He wrapped his hand around the back of my neck. "Come here."

He pulled me flush against him and kissed me. He nipped at my bottom lip until I opened for him. My arms went around his neck as he pushed his tongue into my mouth.

My purse fell off my shoulder with a loud thunk on the floor, but I barely noticed.

We made out right there by his door for a few minutes until I was moaning and trying to wrap my leg around his hip.

Without any warning, he picked me up by grabbing my ass and carried me to the kitchen island. He kissed me a few seconds longer, which I appreciated because he was a really good kisser, before he nudged me away.

"Lie back."

I rested on my elbows as Broderick grabbed the hem of my jeans.

*Am I really going to let him take off my pants?*

This was Broderick after all.

But when I caught a glimpse of anticipation in his eyes, my reservations drifted away.

He yanked my bottoms off in much the same way

Eugene had opened his presents last Christmas. I couldn't help but give a small laugh.

Broderick's eyes flew up to mine, and he smiled. "What's so funny?"

"You remind me of my nephew whenever he gets a gift to unwrap."

"Aw. Except my present is way better than anything he's ever received." With that, he pushed my thighs wide and put his mouth between my legs.

My head fell back against my shoulders. "Oh, yeah." My arms gave out and slid away from me until I was on my back.

I had never been eaten out by a man with a beard before. I would have thought it would be uncomfortable, but it was softer than it looked. And the tiny prickles of it only added sensation to my already-sensitive area.

I didn't know what it was about this man that turned me on so much, but I had to call out a warning sooner than I had expected. "I think I'm going to come."

"Good. That's kind of the goal." He did something with his tongue on my clit, and I almost forgot to ask my next question.

"Don't you want to be inside of me when I do?"

He lifted his head. "Fuck me, Lydia. Stop talking like that, or I'm not going to make it inside you."

"But—"

"No buts. I promised you many little deaths. Now, let me deliver on that."

He pushed two fingers inside me as he sucked on my clit, and that was it. I couldn't hold off any longer, and I exploded all over his face.

I thought I might have literally seen stars because the next thing I was aware of was that his arms were around me, and we were walking toward his bedroom.

"You okay to take off the rest of your clothes, or do you need help?"

"I…I think I'm okay."

"Good," he said and set me on his bed. He yanked his shirt over his head and kicked off his jeans as he opened the drawer on his nightstand.

He was completely naked when he turned around, and I gasped and froze with my shirt halfway over my head.

Broderick went into a semi-defensive pose. "What's wrong?" he asked as he looked around the room.

"I know I'm not a small girl, but you are going to split me in two with that thing."

He immediately relaxed and laughed when he realized I was talking about his giant, enormous cock.

It wasn't the longest I'd ever seen, but it was by far the thickest.

"It's just a dick, Lydia." He stepped closer to me and pulled my shirt the rest of the way off. He reached around and undid my bra with the skill of someone who had a lot of practice. Picking up my hand, he placed it on his erection. "See, he's not going to hurt you."

"Says you."

He took his hand off mine and tugged on one of my nipples.

I moaned.

"Lie back again," he whispered.

I did as he'd said, and as I lay down, he followed, crawling over me.

He sucked one of my nipples into his mouth as he slid his fingers inside me again. "I love how soft you are. Soft and wet. I don't think you have anything to worry about."

I lifted my head. "Huh?"

He laughed. "Never mind." He made a *come here* motion with his fingers, and I whimpered. "Feel good?"

I let my head fall back to the bed. "God, yes."

"That means it's time to let go, babe," he said and pulled my hand from his dick.

He moved my legs to either side of him. "Hey."

I looked into his eyes, and he drove inside me with one steady thrust.

I sucked in a breath as I adjusted to his size, but it took seconds rather than the minutes I had feared.

God, I never knew being this full could feel so good.

I arched my hips. "Fuck me, Broderick."

The corner of his mouth lifted in a half-smile.

"And I've seen how much you work out. You'd better make this good."

He shook his head with a laugh.

But in several smooth moves, he pulled out of me, rolled me onto my hands and knees, and was inside me again.

He grabbed on to my hair and wrapped it around his wrist. "You know what they say?" he said next to my ear.

"What's that?" I panted out.

"The customer is always right."

Pushing my head to the mattress, he slammed into me so hard that I screamed.

## SEVENTEEN

# BRODERICK

I FLIPPED Lydia onto her back after she came again and slowed my pace.

She wildly shook her head back and forth. "I can't anymore, Broderick."

"Can't what?"

She reached up and ran her nails down my chest. "I can't fuck anymore."

I dropped down to my elbows, so I could kiss her. "But you told me I'd better make this good."

"I surrender. You are the king of fucking. But I can't come anymore. My vagina is going to fall off. I regret ever issuing you a challenge."

I pushed her hair off her face and smirked. "Why didn't you just say so?"

"Don't make me leave you here with blue balls."

"Ha. You wouldn't dare."

Before she could answer, I buried my face in her neck and pounded into her like my orgasm depended on it.

I supposed it kind of did.

Lydia moaned and clawed at my back.

"Think you can come again?" I asked.

She laughed in disbelief. "No."

"Want to bet on it?"

She didn't answer.

"If you don't have another orgasm before I leave your body, you can have tomorrow off from training."

"And if you win?"

"You have to train tomorrow."

"That's it?"

I nuzzled her jaw. "Do you like giving head?" I asked and paused for a second.

Her pussy squeezed around me.

"I'll take that as a yes." I nipped at her earlobe. "If I make you climax again, then I also want you to suck me off until I come on your tits."

She groaned low in her throat.

She liked the idea.

I thought for sure she'd tell me no.

Instead, she said, "You've got a deal."

I sat up. "Great. You're going to look so beautiful with my cum on your chest." I licked my thumb.

She met my gaze, determination in her eyes. "Except you're not going to win."

"I guess we'll see about that." I pushed my wet thumb on her clit and slapped it against that swollen nub maybe all of twenty times before her legs clamped down on my hips and her pussy squeezed around my dick.

I grabbed on to her, yanked her hard onto my cock, and came inside her.

"Goddamn it, I love to win."

After tying off the condom and throwing it in the garbage in the corner of my room, I dropped down onto my pillow. I pulled Lydia up beside me and yanked the covers over us.

"You're an arrogant ass," she said into my chest.

My brow furrowed. "I'd like to think I'm confident."

She began to chuckle, which turned into a full-blown laugh within seconds.

"Okay, what's so funny?"

She drew her head back, so I could see her face. "I don't think you want to know."

"Oh, but I do."

"Sometimes, when I was really mad at you, I called you Brode*dick* in my head."

"Nice, Lydia."

"Hey, it's hilarious."

"So now, what are you going to call me?"

She grinned. "Brode*dick*."

I frowned. "But that's the same name."

"But now, I'm going to call you that because I know what you're packing." Her fingers wrapped around me, and I hissed.

"Whoa, whoa, babe. I'm still sensitive."

Her eyes bugged out. "And hard. How are you still hard? We just had sex"—she sat up for a moment to look at my bedside clock—"for almost forty-five minutes."

"I don't follow."

"The average sex session lasts three to seven minutes."

"Oh. So, you're saying having sex with me is a bad thing?" I teased.

"If you were attempting a quickie, then yes."

"It's been a few months. I wanted to make it last." Plus, I'd been thinking about sex with her pretty much since I'd moved in. I hadn't wanted to rush anything.

*And speaking of fantasies…*

I tugged the sheet off her breasts. "I forgot to compliment you on these beauties." I cupped one in my hand and brushed my thumb over the pink bud. "These are even more gorgeous than I pictured in my mind."

"You pictured my breasts in your mind?"

"You know your nipples are constantly hard around me. It's like they're begging me to suck them."

She tilted her head and had a confused smile on her face.

"What?"

"Those are the words Guy Problems used."

I grinned. "They were good words."

"But…"

"But what?"

She shook her head. "Nothing." She rolled her eyes. "I'm imagining things."

I thought maybe she was going to ask if I was Guy Problems. I would tell her the truth, but since she didn't ask, I didn't offer. Plus, I really liked the back-and-forth Guy Problems had with Ask Lydia. And the audience seemed to like it. Who was I to take that away from them?

I was going to need to send in another question soon.

I tugged down the sheet a little further and rolled her on top of me. "What are you imagining?" I kissed her neck. "Me going down on that sweet, sweet pussy again?" I kissed her collarbone. "Me fucking you again?" I scooted down

105

and sucked her nipple in my mouth. Releasing her tip, I looked up at her. "You riding me?" I grabbed on to her hips and yanked her down until she was over my cock. "What are you imagining?" I kissed her long and deep. "You can tell me."

"I want all that."

*Dammit.* So did I.

"Looks like we're in for a long night."

# EIGHTEEN

## LYDIA

I SLOWLY SAT up in the darkness of Broderick's bedroom and waited for my body to start protesting my movements.

After my feet were on the floor, I released the breath I'd been holding and relaxed some.

It made sense that with all the screwing the two of us had done last night, I might have a muscle or two objecting. But I was feeling pretty okay.

I looked over at the clock and saw that it was almost five in the morning.

With a defeated sigh, I stood, and that was when my vagina decided to let me know that all my extracurricular activities didn't sit well with her.

But she was the one who had kept coming at the drop of a hat whenever Broderick touched her. It wasn't my fault she was so sensitive.

A few seconds passed, and I realized that I was still standing there when what I really needed to do was get back home.

I had to use the bathroom and get some coffee in me before we started training.

I found my shirt and bra on the floor next to a sleeping Broderick.

Part of me wanted to slap him for still being out of it. The infuriating guy had kept me up half the night, and soon, he was going to have the audacity to make me run.

I looked down at my vagina, the traitor. We could have been sleeping in this morning.

As I practically limped out of the bedroom, I held in a whimper. More out of tiredness than pain.

I found my pants and underwear in the kitchen and realized I was going to have to put them on before I could walk out into the hall. I tried to get one leg into my underwear and had to stifle a moan. There was the soreness I had been expecting.

I never was one to wish I were a superhero or to have magical powers, but what I wouldn't give to make a temporary door between our two places, so I could simply walk into my apartment from his.

I didn't have time for this.

Next to the door was a coat rack, and I picked through the few articles of clothing hanging there.

*Perfect.*

I slipped on the oversize zip-up hoodie and made sure it was long enough to cover my butt.

I folded my clothes and underwear, grabbed my purse off the floor, and slipped out of the apartment.

When I got into mine—without anyone seeing me, thankfully—I had every intention of making coffee, taking a shower to wash off the sex, and being ready to work out on time.

But as I dropped off my dirty clothes and Broderick's sweatshirt in the hamper in my bedroom, my bed called my name. My numerous pillows and my big, fluffy comforter were too much to resist.

"Fifteen minutes," I lectured myself.

A person could get a surprising amount of rest with a fifteen-minute nap. I set my alarm and crawled into bed, naked.

"Ah," I moaned and pulled my covers up over my head.

---

### BRODERICK

I glanced at my watch for what was probably the fifth time as I paced outside Lydia's apartment. Besides Monday, she'd met me every day in the hall, but it had never taken her this long to show up. She usually beat me to the hallway.

When I'd woken up alone, I'd figured it was no big deal. Lydia had gone home to get ready. But now, I wondered if she was hiding from me.

When was this woman going to understand that she didn't have to be embarrassed about having orgasms in front of me?

I knocked on her door and called her phone a couple of times. It was a repeat of Monday.

I thought I needed to remind her that I'd won the bet last night.

As I had done at the beginning of the week, I jumped

from my balcony to hers. I knocked on the sliding glass door, hoping she would answer from her side, but I couldn't detect any sounds or movements coming from her place. So, I did the inevitable and jimmied the lock.

All was quiet when I entered, so I headed straight for Lydia's room.

I smiled when I saw her buried under her covers with soft snores escaping from her lips.

I lay down on the bed and drew the comforter down from her face.

"Lydia."

She closed her mouth, and her brow furrowed, but she didn't fully wake up.

"Lydia."

Her hand swung out, and she slapped it on my face. "No more sex."

I laughed through her spread fingers. "I'm not here for sex."

Her eyes opened, and she blinked a few times. She noticed my face and yanked her arm back. "Sorry." She rolled onto her back and frowned. "We're at my place."

"Yes, we are. You left me this morning."

She pulled her covers up to her chin and closed her eyes. "I didn't leave you. I came home to get ready, and I fell back asleep."

"It's time to get up. We're wasting precious time."

"I don't wanna."

"Then, you shouldn't have lost the bet," I teased.

She opened one eye and turned her head toward me. "I don't think I can run today. I'm sore."

I shook my head with a smile. As a trainer, I'd heard a

lot of excuses from clients. "You've made it all week. I'm sure you can do one more day. Then, you'll have Saturday and Sunday to sleep in."

"No, you don't understand. I'm not sore from running. I'm sore because your penis ruined my vagina."

*Okay.* I hadn't been expecting her to say that, and I was momentarily at a loss for words. I recalled our night together. Had I missed something? I knew women sometimes said yes when they didn't want to get physical because it was easier. Had I pressured her in some way?

I dropped onto my back. "I really am a dick." I sat up. "I'm sorry."

She chuckled. "I was joking, Brode*dick*." She stretched and yawned. "Not about being sore, but about you ruining my vagina."

I narrowed my eyes at her. "Don't joke about sexual assault, Lydia. It's not funny."

Her eyes widened, and she seemed well and truly awake now. "I'm sorry. That wasn't my intention. I was joking about the size of your dick."

"Oh." My shoulders relaxed. I hoped she didn't ask me why I had jumped to that conclusion.

She placed her hand on my back. "Are you okay?"

"Yeah. Are you?" I smiled in an attempt to lighten the mood and get rid of the awkwardness. "Besides your sore vagina, that is?"

"Tired. Do you always have that much sex?"

"We didn't have sex that much."

Her brow flew up.

I smiled. "You haven't had the proper men love you, Lydia." I put my hand on her thigh. "But since I don't want

111

to cause you any more pain, put on your swimsuit. I still have a bet to cash in, but we can do it without any running."

She sat up enough to grab the front of my T-shirt and pulled me back down to the bed. "I don't need a swimsuit to give you head."

My cock went stiff at the mention of her giving me a blow job.

I patted her hand. "I'm talking about our morning workout."

She smiled coyly at me. "Are you sure? I'd rather fulfill the other part of the bet."

"Nice try. But we're exercising this morning."

"You're a strange man. Forgoing oral sex for working out."

I had to laugh. "You forget that I like exercise almost as much as sex."

"Ugh," she said as she playfully pushed me away. "Get out of my bed."

I jumped up and walked around the bed. "I'm giving you five minutes to meet me in the hall." I slapped her ass over the covers. "Don't make me come back in here and find you."

# NINETEEN

## LYDIA

"WE'RE GOING SWIMMING?" I asked as Broderick unlocked the door to the apartment pool.

I shouldn't have been surprised with what he'd told me to wear, but I hadn't thought we were going swimming in our own building since it wasn't open yet.

"Are you sure we should be doing this? No one is supposed to be in here until nine."

He pushed the door open and stood back, so I could walk in. "I worked it out with management, so we can swim in here early and alone. That way, no one will get in our way when we swim laps."

I set down my towel at the nearest table. "That was nice of them."

Broderick pulled his shirt over his head and kicked off his sandals.

He really had a fantastic body.

I looked down at myself. And I did not.

Last night, it had been semi-dark. You couldn't see all my body's flaws in the shadows. But the pool was surrounded by windows. Windows, windows everywhere. Windows that let in the bright morning sun.

I sighed.

I really did like my body and was proud of my curves, but it didn't stop me from worrying sometimes that guys wouldn't feel the same. Especially guys who looked and worked out like Broderick. Even though I was confident, I still didn't like being made to feel less than.

I mentally rolled my eyes at myself. *So what if he's better-looking than me? It doesn't mean he's a better person than me.*

He tilted his head. "Are you going to take your clothes off?" he asked me. "Or is that what you're swimming in?"

"Last night was nice," I told him.

He scratched his beard. "It was more than nice. I think your ruined vagina can attest to that."

I laughed. "I'm glad you can joke about that now."

He smiled. "Me too." He stepped closer and pushed my hair behind my ear. "But that's not why you brought last night up."

I grabbed his hand and clutched it between both of mine. "I just want you to know that if it doesn't happen again and you want to go back to…whatever we were before that, I'll understand."

He stepped back and grinned. "Take off your clothes, Karels. I've already seen you naked," he said and jumped into the pool.

I gasped. "I don't know what you're talking about," I yelled when he came up for air.

"You're worried I'm going to judge you on how you look. But I'm not going to do that."

"Everyone judges," I pointed out.

"Yeah, some more than others."

*Was that directed at me?*

"Fine." I pulled one arm through a sleeve and then another. Since I was doing this, I wished I were at least wearing a sexy swimsuit. It was a basic black two-piece. Very boring.

Broderick swam closer and splashed me. "Hurry up."

"Eek." I put my hand up to cover my face. "What's the hurry?" I finished undressing and put my clothes next to my towel.

I turned around to see Broderick staring at me.

Snapping my fingers a couple of times, I said his name.

He looked up to my face. "What?"

I smiled. "I asked you what the hurry was."

"I want to kiss your poor pussy and make it feel better."

"Well then, I don't know what I'm waiting for."

---

I stared at my computer screen and tried to conjure up the words for my Track Lydia article.

But every time I thought of my assignment, I thought of Broderick. And then I thought about him picking me up, setting me on the edge of the pool, pulling the bottom half of my swimsuit off, and giving me the most excellent orgasm.

I couldn't stop picturing his swim trunks molded to his hard-on. I hadn't even been able to return the favor and deliver on the other half of our bet because we were cutting it close to his first client of the day.

If I didn't concentrate on my job, I was going to get myself worked up, and I would never get this article written.

And I needed to get it done. It was my second article but my first to turn in since my visit from Eve. If I could make demands of my boss, I was going to need to do my part.

I closed my eyes, centered my thoughts, and concentrated on my morning workouts that week.

I took a deep breath and opened my eyes. I could do this.

After my introduction last week, I bet you are all wondering if I survived my first week of training.

I'm here to tell you, I have.

But that doesn't mean it's been easy. Thankfully, I have some help from a personal trainer…

---

I sat back and reread my article. I fixed my spelling and grammar mistakes and went through it again. I was pretty satisfied with my work. I had written about my training without making it boring, and I had mentioned Broderick a couple of times, like I'd promised. I hoped that when this whole thing was over, the magazine helped bring him some new clients.

With a weight being lifted off my shoulders, I uploaded my article to *Afterglow*'s cloud drive and grabbed my phone.

I found my friend Phoebe in my messages.

> Me: After today, I need a drink. You up for it?

Within seconds, I got a response.

Phoebe: Bad day?

I smiled. *Not the* whole *day.*

Me: Not necessarily bad. I finished my first week of training and sent in my article to my boss. I want to relax and have a drink. So, are you in?

Phoebe: As if you have to ask.

Me: You want to come over after work?

Phoebe: I only worked half a day. I can be there in fifteen minutes. Unless you need to keep working.

I really should do some stuff for Ask Lydia before I called it a day, but I could make up some of that tomorrow.

Me: Fuck it. I'll see you in fifteen.

Phoebe: I'm already walking out the door.

Since I had a few minutes before Phoebe arrived, I opened my Ask Lydia email. Immediately, I noticed there was a new message from Guy Problems.

*Dear Lydia,*

*Again, thank you for the advice. I considered asking someone else out on a date, but then I remembered you said not to force anything. And while I can't forget about my neighbor, I also can't force interest for someone else.*

*Perhaps that will change in the future, but at the moment, I decided to act on my feelings and took my neighbor to bed. (Don't worry. She was very willing.)*

*I'm sure that it seems like everything has worked out between us, but I have yet to bring up the questionable things she said about me behind my back. And now, I'm not sure how to bring it up. I don't want to start a fight because I think I might like my neighbor more than just sexually. Any advice is appreciated.*

*Sincerely,*

*Guy Problems*

# TWENTY

## LYDIA

I HANDED my laptop to Phoebe, so she could read my latest email from Guy Problems.

When she was finished, she burst out laughing. "I love this guy."

I took my computer away from her and set it back on my desk before she knocked it on the floor.

She tilted her auburn head. "Don't you?"

I shrugged and sat back down on the couch. "I think he's just messing with me at this point."

She pointed her wineglass at me. "Or he likes the attention. I've seen the comments."

I picked up my own glass and took a long sip. "Yeah, it could be that too."

"Oh my God," she said.

"What?"

"You want him to be flirting with you?"

I sat up straight. "No, I don't."

She pushed my leg with her foot. "You said all those women were silly for falling for a guy they had never seen."

I sagged back against the couch. "If I tell you something, do you promise not to judge?"

Phoebe smiled as she took a drink of her wine and shook her head. "I can't promise that because then I would be lying."

"I appreciate the honesty, but next time, just lie to me."

She laughed. "If you say so. Now, spill."

"I think Guy Problems might be my neighbor."

Her mouth dropped open. "The neighbor who you don't like but decided you do like enough to let train you?"

I looked away. "Also, the neighbor I had sex with last night."

She gasped, and I looked back at her.

"Lydia Karels, you slut." She lifted her glass in the air. "I approve of this one hundred percent."

I clinked my glass against hers. "Thanks, I guess."

"Tell me everything. Are you going to start dating him?" She shook her head. "Never mind. You don't date."

"I date."

"But you never get serious."

She had me there. I usually ended things after a few months, and I didn't really understand why. I hadn't been hurt by an ex, nor had I had a bad experience from my parents. They were divorced but had actually remained friends, and both were remarried and happy. As far as being a kid from a divorced family, I had the best-case scenario.

I thought it came down to liking my independence too much. And I'd never found a man I wanted to give that up for.

"I'm sure I will one day." When I thought about the distant future, I did picture myself in a serious relationship.

"Eh. He's probably not *the one* anyway. But I still don't know what he looks like. Is he on Instagram? Facebook? Twitter?"

I shrugged. "I don't know."

"Lydia, you can't have sex with someone before looking at their social media. They might have a secret lover or something. For someone who made a lot of assumptions about him, I am shocked you didn't look at his social media."

I sheepishly took a sip of my wine. "I'm not a stalker."

Grabbing her phone off my coffee table, she asked, "What's his last name?"

I shook my head. "I'm not telling."

I didn't want her looking him up because it kind of felt wrong if I wasn't going to friend or follow him. But I also didn't want to know what I would find, and I didn't want to see something that would make me feel differently about him.

I picked up the pillow beside me and screamed into it.

"What was that about?" Phoebe asked.

I dropped the pillow into my lap and whined, "I think I might like him." I looked at my friend. "It's only been a week. How can I change my feelings so fast?"

"They say there's a thin line between love and hate. But I wouldn't worry about it. You have sex brain."

"Sex brain?"

"Yeah. It's a form of brain fog, revolving around the guy you had sex with. You can't think straight, and you don't recognize your feelings. Don't worry. It won't last."

"I like that excuse."

"Since you won't let me look up your neighbor, why

don't you tell me why you think he's Guy Problems? All the neighbor stuff?"

"Yeah. Mostly."

"Okay, but what about the stuff behind his back? Do you go around, talking about him to your neighbors?"

I frowned. She had a good point. "No. I don't really talk much to any of my neighbors on a regular basis." I picked at the corner of my pillow.

"I'm sorry."

I lifted my eyes. "Why? You didn't do anything."

"I totally burst your bubble."

I sighed. "It's okay. I mean, what are the chances that he would have found my magazine and sent me a message?"

"He doesn't know what you do?"

"He does, but we didn't discuss it until after the first email from Guy Problems came in."

"Bummer." She stuck out her lower lip.

"Yeah, it's probably for the best."

"So, what are you going to tell Guy Problems?"

"Ugh. I have no idea. Now that I know it's not Broderick, I do worry he's doing the whole back-and-forth for attention."

"Can you ignore it?"

"I can ask Eve."

Phoebe curled her lip at the mention of my boss. "She's going to eat that shit up."

On that thought, I downed the rest of my glass. "You're right."

"More wine?" Phoebe asked.

"Yes, please."

My friend got up and went to get the bottle we had left

in the kitchen when music from next door started pounding through my and Broderick's shared wall.

Phoebe turned around and grinned at me.

Alarm bells went off in my head. "What are you thinking?"

Instead of answering, she ran out my door.

"Phoebe? What the hell?"

Unfortunately, it wasn't until I heard Broderick's music turn down that I realized what she had done.

I flew off the couch and out into the hall. I stopped when I saw her standing in front of Broderick's door.

"Hey, uh, my friend and I can hear your music. Do you mind turning it down a little?" Phoebe tried to sound innocent, but I knew she had done it to see what my neighbor looked like.

I stepped forward until I could see Broderick standing in his apartment. He had his shirt off and was leaning against the doorframe with one arm over his head. He looked delicious, but the sexiest thing about him was that his polite smile turned into a full grin when he saw me.

"Hey, Lydia."

"Hey." I looped my arm through Phoebe's. "Your music isn't that loud. Don't worry about it."

"Or you can come over and join us?" Phoebe said.

Broderick smiled and dropped his arm. "I have another client coming soon."

"That's a shame." She arched onto her tiptoes. "So, does that mean you're working out in there alone?"

"I am. But hey, if you're ever looking for a personal trainer, I can give you my card."

"Will I get all the benefits that Lydia does?"

Broderick's eyes shot to mine, and I dropped my head in my hand.

"Sorry, I don't get involved with clients."

"But what about Lydia?"

"Lydia is my friend, who I am doing a favor for."

I looked up at him and smiled.

Phoebe leaned close to him. "Excellent answer."

He looked at me like he didn't know what to do with my friend. Truthfully, I didn't know either.

"We'll let you go back to your workout," I said and tugged on Phoebe's arm. "Let's go."

"Bye, ladies."

"Bye, Broderick," Phoebe said with a finger wave.

"Bye."

Broderick stepped forward and pulled me in for a kiss. "Call me later, okay?"

"Okay," I said, stunned.

Broderick shut his door, and Phoebe fell back against the wall.

"And now, I'm pregnant." She fanned her face. "He is so hot. I don't care how mad he ever made me. I would hate-fuck him so good."

A chuckle sounded from the other side of the door.

I grabbed Phoebe's hand and tugged her toward my place. "No more wine for you."

# TWENTY-ONE

## LYDIA

I FIDDLED WITH MY PHONE, unsure of what to do.

After dragging Phoebe from Broderick's place, we had gone out for dinner, and now, I was home, lying in bed, wondering if I should call Broderick, like he'd asked.

I opted for sending him a text instead.

> Me: Hope your night went well. Sorry about my friend.

And so I didn't stare at my phone, I picked up my computer from my nightstand and composed my response to Guy Problems.

*Dear Guy Problems,*

*I'm glad that things are working out well with you and your neighbor, and I'm glad that you didn't force interest in someone else.*

*However, I am concerned that you have not been completely honest with your neighbor. I fear that if you continue to build a relationship without bringing up your concerns, they will cause more trouble later than they will if you brought it up now.*

*Perhaps you've even convinced yourself that it's not a big deal, but once the honeymoon phase wears off, you might come to resent her. And maybe you won't, but she might have issues with trusting you if you keep it to yourself.*

*Wishing you all the luck!*

*Lydia*

I reread both the message from Guy Problems and my response, and I had to wonder if the readers would still be excited to see what he was up to. Maybe they would forget him once they knew he was taken.

I uploaded both question and response into the cloud drive before answering another reader's email.

It was getting late, and after a certain time, it was harder for me to concentrate.

Besides, there was only so much work I could do while pretending that I wasn't waiting for Broderick to message me back.

With a sigh, I turned off my laptop and set it on my nightstand.

This was one of the reasons I wasn't a big fan of relationships. I had slept with my neighbor once, and now, I was lying around, waiting to hear back from him, as if he were suddenly the center of my world.

He was just a guy I'd had sex with, and I hated that I was staring at my phone again, trying to figure out what to do about him. I should be doing my own thing and not caring whether he texted me back or not.

But I also didn't want to be rude, so I asked myself what I would do if it was a friend, and I pretended Broderick was Phoebe. Since he had told me to call him, I decided I would leave him one more message.

> Me: Headed to bed. We'll talk tomorrow. If not, have a good weekend, and I'll see you bright and early on Monday.

I hit Send and smiled. My message was totally casual, and I'd let him know that I was cool if we didn't see each other until Monday. And that when we did see each other, then it was because of my training.

"*Ugh.*" I shouldn't have to make sure my text sounded casual. I was over this.

I turned my phone on silent and practically slammed it down on my nightstand. A handsome face and sexy green eyes had me all twisted up inside like I was in high school again.

I needed to forget about him.

I turned my back to my cell and clicked the power button on the remote. I found a true crime show on TV and settled in, determined not to think about Broderick the rest of the night.

---

The next morning, I didn't get to sleep in like I had wanted to. Apparently, my body was used to getting up early, like I had all week. But the good thing was, I didn't have to work out, so I could sit around in my pajamas for a bit.

I grabbed my phone from my nightstand and was disappointed to see that Broderick hadn't messaged me back at all last night. But I was happy to see the situation for what it was. Not only was I not a big fan of relationships, but even if I were, Broderick and I were too different.

After letting myself lie in bed and mindlessly scroll through social media for way too long, I got up and made myself some breakfast. And after taking a shower, I treated myself to a latte from Caribou. I hadn't gone as much this past week as I normally did, and I didn't want the place to forget about me.

When I got back home, I could hear music playing at Broderick's place. It wasn't particularly loud, but it did tell me that he was home. I couldn't help but wonder what he had done the night before, and I really needed to stop thinking about him.

It was a good thing I had plans for the day. I needed to get some work done since I had quit early the day before, and as a reward for working out all week, I had a massage scheduled in the afternoon. I almost got relaxed, just thinking about it.

But until then, I opened up my regular work email to see that Eve had emailed me in the middle of the night.

*Lydia,*

*Great job on the article. I'm glad things are working out with your neighbor training you. I can't wait to see how you do at the triathlon.*

. . .

I gave my computer the finger. I hated that she was talking to me like she hadn't coerced me into doing the assignment. But I continued on.

*The subscribers are also really into Guy Problems. I already read your most recent response to him, and it is good. I will post it, but if he writes back again, I was thinking you could somehow open up a dialogue with him to keep him writing in. The readers will eat it up.*

    *Keep up the good work!*
    *Eve*

*Ugh.* She made me feel sick to my stomach. I hated that I had a great job that I loved but a boss who sucked. I had never been Eve's biggest fan, and I had heard rumors of things she had done to others in the past, but I'd never imagined she would be this manipulative. It even made me not want to do my job.

It took all my mental energy to convince myself that I was doing my work that morning for the readers and not to pad Eve's bank account. The good part was, I completely put Broderick out of my mind, and I kept myself busy until it was time for me to leave for my appointment.

# TWENTY-TWO

# BRODERICK

SATURDAYS, I did an online class, and I had a few clients that I saw in the morning. But I did try not to book my whole day. One thing I had learned from my previous job was to make sure I had more in my life than just my work and to give myself some downtime. Even though I loved being active, I still appreciated an occasional session of vegging in front of the TV.

That afternoon, I was paying some bills and cross-referencing my finances. I had never been big into math or accounting stuff, so this had been the biggest hurdle in making my own business. Soon, I hoped to hire a full-time accountant to keep the stuff straight for me.

Since my apartment was silent so I could concentrate, I easily heard voices in the hall and the knock on Lydia's door.

I hadn't talked to her since yesterday. I hoped she would call me last night and that maybe we could get together again, but she only sent me a text. And since my phone didn't ring, I didn't hear it last night. I'd only seen her messages that morning, and I hadn't figured out what to say back to her yet.

Her texts had been a little unemotional or distant to someone who'd had his dick in her the night before. I wasn't sure if that was the nice way of saying to leave her alone or what was going on, and I was too old to play high school games.

I did notice that Lydia hadn't answered her door, and I went to look out my peephole to see who was there. But before I could reach my own door, there was a knock.

I opened it to find Lydia's brother, who I had met very briefly the other night when he came to pick up his kids. Eugene and Tabitha were with him today too.

"Hi. I don't know if you remember me. I'm Lydia's brother," he said with a nervous smile on his face.

"Yes, Eli. Is there something I can help you with?" I looked down at the kids. "Hey, Eugene. Hey, Tabitha."

"Hi, Broderick." Eugene beamed up at me.

"Do you know where my sister is?" Eli asked.

"Sorry, I don't."

"Dammit," he muttered under his breath. "Okay, kids, let's go." He looked at me. "Will you tell my sister that I'm looking for her?"

"I'll do that."

"Thanks." Eli looked weary and stressed.

"Is there anything I can help you with?"

He laughed without humor. "Know any last-minute babysitters? My wife's mom is in the hospital. They had to take her there by ambulance. I sent my wife to the hospital and told her I would meet her there after I found someone to take the kids. But my mom and stepdad are out of town, and so are my dad and stepmom. And all our friends are busy." He rubbed his forehead.

I felt for the guy. "I don't know any babysitters, but if you want to leave the kids here with me until Lydia gets home, I'd be happy to help."

His head snapped up. "Really?" The relief in his eyes was almost palpable.

"Really. I was just sitting around, paying bills, anyway. Babysitting gives me a good excuse to stop."

"Oh my God. You are a lifesaver." Eli looked down at his kids. "Are you two okay with staying here with Lydia's neighbor for a little while?"

"Sure," Tabitha said.

"We get to play video games," Eugene said.

"I'll take that as a yes," Eli said.

I opened my door further. "Come on in, kids."

They ran past their dad and me and into my apartment.

"Seriously, thank you so much. I will continue to call my sister until she answers to let her know that my kids are with you."

"No rush." I didn't want him to worry that he was inconveniencing me. The last time I had been with them, I'd had fun with Eugene, and Tabitha seemed like a good kid.

He pulled out his wallet and gave me a card. "My cell number is on there. Please call me if you need anything."

I looked at the card. "Will do."

He started backing away and raised a hand in a wave. "Thank you again. I'm very grateful."

I waved back. "You're welcome."

Eli pivoted on his heel and sprinted toward the stairs.

I closed the door and turned around. "Okay, what do you want to do first?"

"Play video games," Eugene said at the same time Tabitha said, "Watch Netflix."

She looked at her brother. "I'm older, so I get to choose."

"Nuh-uh. Those aren't the rules."

I could see this turning into a big fight, so I clapped my hands together. "How about we do both?"

Tabitha crossed her arms. "How are you going to do that? I only see one TV."

---

## LYDIA

I left the spa, feeling great. I had caught up on all my work before I went, and I'd gotten my massage from my favorite masseur. I still wasn't happy with my boss, but I decided that could wait until Monday. I was going to enjoy the rest of my weekend.

On my way to the spa, some friends had called me and asked me if I wanted to go out to a club. I had said yes and was looking forward to seeing my friends. About three-fourths of them were now in either a serious relationship, engaged, or married. I supposed that was what happened once you hit thirty. But it was harder for all of us to find the time to do stuff, and sometimes, it came down to last-minute plans.

Once I was in the car, I checked my phone before I took

off to make sure that nothing had changed. That was also the downfall of planning things late. Someone could cancel at the last minute.

There was nothing from my friends, but it looked like my brother had called me a few times, and I had at least one voice mail. He had also texted me, but he didn't tell me what was going on. He'd only told me to call him back ASAP.

Once I was on the road and my phone connected to my car's Bluetooth, I tried calling my brother back, but he didn't answer. I really hated when people didn't tell me what was wrong in text, and I loathed voice mail for some reason, but I reluctantly listened to mine. My brother knew how much I disliked it, so it must be important.

"Hey, where are you? It's an emergency. I need you to watch the kids. Faith's mother is in the hospital. We don't know anything yet, except that she called Faith to say that she had to call for an ambulance. Faith already went to the hospital, but I don't want to take the kids since I don't know how long we will be waiting. And Mom and Dad are both out of town. Can you babysit? Call me back, please."

*"Oh no."*

I tried calling my brother again, but there was still no answer. I tapped my steering wheel and debated on if I should call my sister-in-law. I didn't want to interrupt her if she was with her family—or God forbid, if she was grieving. But I wanted her to know that I was ready to take the kids for them.

After going back and forth with myself, I gave her a call. She didn't answer either. I hoped that wasn't a bad sign.

Even though my parents were out of town, I was pretty sure my brother would've told my mom what was going on, so I called her.

Thankfully, she answered right away.

"Lydia, where have you been? Your brother's been trying to reach you."

I winced because saying I had been at the spa sounded horrible when someone was in the hospital.

"I know. I had an appointment, and my phone was on silent. I can't get ahold of Eli. Do you know what he did with the kids?"

"Roman and I are on our way back from Iowa. Tabitha and Eugene can come spend the night with us."

That was great and all, but that didn't tell me where they were now.

"So, the kids are still with Eli?"

"Oh, no. He said he left them with your neighbor. Some guy named Rick?"

*Oh shit.*

"His name is Broderick, Mom."

"Yeah, that's it. He took the kids until you got home."

I couldn't believe my brother had left Eugene and Tabitha with Broderick. We weren't even in a relationship, and he was watching my niece and nephew. How awkward.

"I'll text or call when we get close to your place, so you can have the kids ready," my mom continued on, oblivious to my panic.

"Do you know what's going on with Faith's mom?" I asked because that was the really important issue here.

"I'm sorry, honey. I can't quite remember what Eli said.

I think they're going to take her to surgery, but I don't know when."

Surgery wasn't good, but at least that meant she was still alive and hopefully stable.

"Thanks for the update. I'm almost home. I'll see you when you get here. Drive safe."

## TWENTY-THREE

## BRODERICK

"GET HIM, BRODERICK. GET HIM," Eugene said.

I laughed at the little guy's enthusiasm. It was fun, playing video games with him.

"Tabitha, are you doing okay in there?"

I'd set up a little spot in my workout room for Tabitha to watch Netflix on my laptop. I had tried to keep her in the living room with us, but she had complained that we were too loud.

"I'm fine. Do you have any snacks?" she called back.

"Uh…"

My lack of an answer was drowned out by the pounding of footsteps in the hall and a loud knock at my door. I smiled because it had to be Lydia.

As soon as I answered the door, I said, "I'm so glad you're here. They just asked me for snacks."

She ignored me and pushed her way inside. I noticed she was out of breath. She must have run the whole way up.

"Hey, Aunt Lydia."

Eugene smiled at her, and I could see the relief wash over her face.

Tabitha came out to the living room. "Hey, Aunt Lydia."

"Are you two okay?" she asked her niece and nephew.

Tabitha shrugged. "I'm hungry."

"Right," I said. I leaned closer to Lydia and whispered, "Do you have any snacks for them? Because I don't really keep junk food in my house."

She smiled slightly for the first time since arriving. "Of course you don't." She clapped her hands together. "You guys ready to come over to my place?"

"I want to stay here," Eugene said. "Broderick and I are playing a game again."

"And I'm watching a movie," Tabitha added.

Lydia looked stressed. "You can watch a movie at my place," she told her niece and turned to her nephew. "And you can just play video games with Broderick another time."

"Hey, can I talk to you in private?" I asked her.

"Sure."

Since my apartment had an open concept and there were two sets of eyes on us, I led her to my bedroom and closed the door. When I turned around, I saw her staring at my bed. Thankfully, I had made it that morning.

"I didn't want to say this in front of Tabitha and Eugene, but you're more than welcome to stay here. Or if you want me to keep Eugene while you take Tabitha to your place, I can do that too."

Her back stiffened. "They're not your responsibility," she said with a bit of force.

I figured she was probably stressed out with what was

going on with her family, so I wasn't going to take it personally.

"I know that. But you are my neighbor and my friend, and friends help each other out."

Her shoulders relaxed. "Where is Tabitha watching the movie?"

"I set up my computer for her in the other bedroom. She and Eugene started fighting about who got the TV almost right away."

"My brother and sister-in-law would probably disapprove of you not making them share, but as their aunt and fellow babysitter, I totally approve of your strategy."

I laughed.

"Why didn't you just have her watch TV in your bedroom?" Lydia looked across from my bed, where my dresser sat. "Oh man, you don't have a TV in your room either. Somehow, I missed that the other night."

"According to the experts, it's not healthy. And you were a little preoccupied when you were in here last."

She blushed.

"Also, I haven't washed my sheets since you and I had sex, and it just didn't seem right to let your innocent niece lie on my bed."

I thought her cheeks turned redder, and I had to hide my smile.

"Well, I don't care if it's unhealthy. I love falling asleep to the television."

I guessed we weren't going to talk about the fact that we'd slept together. It was understandable. She was under some stress.

"So, do you want to go and get something for the kids to eat? Or I can go if you give me your key."

"No, I'll go. I'll be faster."

I opened the door and walked out of my bedroom.

"Were you guys kissing in there?" Eugene asked.

I had to laugh at the kid's frankness. "No, we weren't. We were talking."

Eugene's brow furrowed. "Oh. When my mom and dad close their bedroom door, it's usually because they're kissing."

"They're not kissing, dork," Tabitha said. "They're having sex."

"Oh my God. Please stop talking about your parents like that," Lydia said with horror. "And, Tabitha, you are not supposed to know what sex is."

"I don't know what sex is, Aunt Lydia." Eugene smiled. "You can tell me."

"No." She stomped toward the door. "I'll be right back with some food."

I turned to Eugene. "Want to keep playing our game?"

"I want to know what sex is."

"Not going to happen," I told him. I put my hand up before Tabitha could say anything. "Not a word."

She shrugged and went back into the exercise room.

A couple of minutes later, Lydia came back. "Snack time," she called.

Both kids ran to the kitchen.

Hopefully, this would get them to stop talking about sex. Even better, they would forget they'd ever tried to have the conversation with us.

Lydia dumped all the food on my kitchen island and

stepped over to me while the kids picked what they wanted to eat.

"Your nephew wanted me to tell him what S-E-X was. Your brother isn't paying me enough for all this."

"How much is my brother paying you?"

"Nothing."

"Ah. I think that's where you went wrong. Next time, charge double."

I frowned. "Two times zero is zero."

She rolled her eyes. "You know what I mean."

"If we're lucky, there won't be a next time."

"Even better."

## TWENTY-FOUR

## LYDIA

BRODERICK and I managed to entertain the kids long enough until we fed them pizza—again—for dinner. We had decided to stay at Broderick's place so Eugene could play video games. And right after the dishes went in the dishwasher, my mom and stepdad showed up.

"Grandma!" Eugene yelled when he saw my mom.

I walked over and gave her a hug. "Hey, Mom. I'm glad you're here." I stepped back. "Hey, Roman."

"Hey, kiddo."

I smiled. He'd been calling me that since he and my mom started dating when I was in middle school.

"Mom, Roman, this is Broderick."

Broderick stepped forward and shook hands with each of them.

"Thank you for babysitting," my mom said.

"It's the least I could do."

Mom looked at me. "What a nice young man."

I rolled my eyes. "Mom."

She was always trying to set me up with someone.

"Have you heard from Eli?" I asked her.

"Yes. About fifteen minutes ago. Faith's mom fell. She swears she didn't lose consciousness, but they still did a CT scan of her head. It came back clear. Unfortunately, she broke her hip and will have to have surgery tomorrow to fix it. She's awake and in pain, but overall, she's doing well."

I breathed a sigh of relief. When I'd heard that Faith's mom had to go to the hospital, I'd imagined a heart attack or a stroke. When I'd heard surgery earlier, I'd immediately thought of all the times I'd heard someone had to get stents put in their hearts. Not that a fall wasn't serious, but I was glad to hear her heart and brain were in the clear.

"I'm so glad she's going to be okay." I looked around. "Anyway, we just finished dinner, so you don't have to worry about feeding the kids. Do you want the leftover pizza for tomorrow?"

Mom shook her head. "No, you keep it."

I looked at Broderick. "Did the kids come with anything that they need to take with them?"

"No."

"Looks like we'll be stopping at their house to pick up clothes and toothbrushes," Roman said. "Shall we get a move on?"

"Let's go, kids," my mom said. "Put your shoes on. You've taken up enough of Broderick's and Lydia's time." She winked at me.

*Ugh, Mom.*

Tabitha and Eugene did as they had been told, and the four of them filed out the door.

"Thanks again, Broderick," my mom said to him.

"No problem. But I'm telling Eli that I'm charging him a fee next time."

Mom laughed and waved good-bye.

The door closed, and then it was just the two of us.

I wasn't really sure what to say to Broderick. The last time we had been alone, he'd been eating me out down by the pool. It seemed awkward between us now.

"Do you want me to take the pizza home?"

His brow lifted in question.

"I don't know if your fridge has an anti-pizza feature or something like that."

He laughed and stepped forward. "I don't want the pizza to go home. I'd like the pizza to stay right here with me."

I put my arms around his neck. "Oh, really?"

"Oh, yes." He brushed his lips across mine. "In fact, I really wanted pizza last night, but the pizza didn't call me."

I smiled. "But the pizza did text."

"I saw that this morning. And as much as I wanted pizza for breakfast, I had to work."

I slid my hands down his muscular chest. "It's probably a good thing you waited to have pizza tonight because it was still sore last night."

"So, does that mean the pizza is okay with me taking it to my bedroom right now?"

"Pizza is more than okay with it."

Broderick bent down and threw me over his shoulder as I yelped in surprise.

"Just to be clear, you know you're the pizza, right?" he asked.

I laughed. "Yes, I know."

He carried me to his bedroom and gently threw me on the bed. I began undressing as soon as I landed while I watched him strip out of his clothes and tried not to drool.

I couldn't believe I got to touch this handsome man all over.

As soon as we were both naked, I crawled over to him and sucked his cock into my mouth.

This time, it was Broderick's turn to yelp.

"Oh God, Lydia, that feels amazing."

I wasn't big on giving head and never understood why some women liked it so much, but the noises coming out of Broderick's mouth were such a turn-on.

And he didn't complain once that I couldn't get him in my mouth all the way. He seemed to like it, no matter what I was doing.

I sucked the tip and circled my tongue around it before popping him out of my mouth. "Let me know when you're close, okay?"

"Okay," he panted.

His eyes were squeezed closed, and I had to smile.

I gave his balls some love before I went back to his big, gorgeous dick. I pushed him to the back of my throat just to see how far I could go. I was almost there, but it was hard for me to keep it up, so I used my hand to work on the part of him I couldn't fit inside.

His breathing started getting shallower, and he kept cursing under his breath.

I could feel myself getting wet between my legs. This was the most turned on I'd ever been at giving a blow job, and I reached down and flicked my clit.

I continued to rub my swollen nub as I sucked on Broderick. I was getting so close to an orgasm that I was beginning to worry I was going to come before he did.

But just in time it seemed, he cupped the back of my head and said, "I'm going to come."

I sat up and jerked him with my free hand until he came all over my chest. As soon as he groaned in the throes of his climax, I let myself explode too.

Keeping my eyes open while the force of my pleasure coursed through my body was one of the hardest things to do, but I didn't want to miss a second of watching the beautiful show that was Broderick's ecstasy.

When he opened his eyes, he smiled down on me. "Fuck, I wish I could take a picture. Your tits are amazing."

"Is that why you wanted to come on them?"

"Hell yeah. I know it's not PC, but I like the thought of a part of me covering them, as if to say, *These belong to me.*"

My pussy clenched even though I'd just had an orgasm.

I swiped my finger through his cum and lifted it to my lips. "Mmm."

"Holy shit."

"Maybe you have the right idea about eating healthy because I like the way you taste."

"Lydia," he groaned. "I think you're trying to kill me." He grabbed my other hand, which was still between my thighs, and brought it to his mouth. "I love the way you taste too. Now, I want you to sit back on the pillows, so I can eat your pussy while I stare at your chest. Does that work for you?"

He didn't have to ask me twice.

## TWENTY-FIVE

## LYDIA

AFTER BRODERICK GAVE me another orgasm with his mouth, he carried me to the shower, so I could wash all of him off of me. What he didn't know was that I'd snapped a picture of my breasts. I didn't know if I would ever share it with him, but I had it just in case I wanted to.

He pulled out big, fluffy towels for us once we were both clean and led me back to his bedroom. When he dropped his to the floor, I saw that he was hard again.

I licked my lips.

He pulled me into his arms and kissed me as we fell on the mattress. "How sore are you? I really want to make love to you, but I don't want to hurt you."

"I'll only be hurt if you don't get inside me."

The corner of his mouth lifted in a sexy smile, and I kissed him. I rolled us over, so his back was facing the bed, and I leaned over him.

"Condoms?"

He pointed to the nightstand. "In the drawer."

I pulled a couple out and ripped one open before rolling it down his cock. I couldn't wait to feel him inside me again.

I quickly straddled his hips and looked down at him. "Is it okay that I'm on top?"

"You're joking, right?"

"Consent goes both ways, buddy. Some guys don't like it."

He reached up and rubbed my nipples with his thumbs. "You can ride me anytime, Lydia. Anytime at all." He pulled me down with one hand as he held his dick with the other at my center. As I slowly sank down on him, he said, "And that's *lover* to you. We're way past buddies."

I laughed, but it quickly morphed into a gasp when he was fully seated inside me.

I gave my nether regions a moment to adjust and then started rotating my hips. I experimented a little until I found what felt the best.

"Damn, that feels good," I whispered.

"For me too," he said with a groan.

I loved feeling so full, and when I ground my pelvis on his to add friction to my clit, it was magic.

Letting myself go, I rode Broderick until we both came, and I collapsed on top of him.

"That was amazing."

He laughed and rubbed my back. "For me too. But I should probably get rid of the condom."

"Right."

I reluctantly slid off him and dropped onto my side. Broderick threw away the rubber and cuddled me from behind. I closed my eyes, enjoying the feel of my post-orgasmic bliss and the warmth of him behind me, and I was ready to fall asleep when my phone rang from the other room.

I was prepared to ignore it until I remembered that I'd had plans with my friends that I had forgotten to cancel.

"Oh crap." I flung back the covers and raced toward my phone before whoever was calling me got my voice mail.

"Hello?" I answered and hurried back to Broderick's bed, where it was warm.

"Hey, girl," Phoebe said from the other end of the line. "Are you ready to par-tay?"

Broderick grinned at me when I entered. "You should run naked like that more often."

I smiled, shook my head, and climbed in beside him.

"Um…about that."

He pulled me back into his arms and cupped my breast.

"Oh no. You're canceling. Now? I was just going to come and pick you up."

"I'm sorry I didn't call you earlier. Family emergency."

"Oh God. No, that's fine. I wouldn't have remembered to call me either. Is everything okay?"

I filled her in on my sister-in-law's mother and the last-minute babysitting with my neighbor.

"And now, you would rather bone Broderick. I totally understand. I'd rather bone Broderick too. Not that I don't love you and our other friends."

He started laughing behind me. He was trying to be quiet, but I could feel his whole body shaking.

"Um, just so you know, he can hear you."

"Oh." She sounded happy, not surprised. "Tell him hi for me."

Broderick leaned forward. "Hi, Phoebe."

"Give my friend lots of orgasms, okay? She deserves it."

"Jeez, Phoebe." I could feel my face heating.

"I already did," Broderick said back into the phone.

"You dirty, dirty wench." Phoebe laughed. "The sun hasn't even gone down yet."

I smiled. "What can I say?"

"Since you already got your freak on, are you sure you don't want to go out with us?"

Broderick ran his hand down my side. "I'll understand if you want to go," he whispered.

I looked back at him and kissed him. "Thanks, but I think I'll pass. Will you tell everyone I'm sorry?"

"There's no need to be sorry. Life happens. We'll talk later, okay?"

"Okay. Have fun tonight."

"Will do."

"Bye."

The call ended, and I set my phone on the nightstand. I turned around and faced Broderick.

"Are you sure you don't want to go?" he asked me.

"I'm sure. Are you trying to get rid of me?"

"Hell no. But I don't want you to feel like you have to stay."

"I'm here because I want to be."

He grinned. "Good. The night is still early. Whatever should we do?"

"Well, if you had a television in here, we could watch TV," I teased.

"Or we could have sex again."

I smiled. "That is another idea."

He kissed my shoulder. "I told you having a TV in the bedroom wasn't healthy."

## TWENTY-SIX

## BRODERICK

THE FOLLOWING FRIDAY, Lydia and I were headed back to our apartment building after training while I tried not to stare at her butt when she walked ahead of me into the building.

The two of us had been having a lot of sex this past week, and I couldn't seem to get enough of her.

She looked over her shoulder. "Are you staring at my ass?"

"You know it."

"I don't think that's appropriate for trainers to do."

I winced at her words, and she stopped walking.

She put her hands on my chest. "Hey, I was just joking. You have been nothing but professional when it's training time. I just thought that since we were done for the day, we could go back to being just Broderick and Lydia."

I cupped her neck and kissed her. "You did nothing wrong. Just a bad memory popped into my head."

"About me?"

I smiled and shook my head. "No."

"Do you want to talk about it?"

I knew that if we continued to see each other, I would have to eventually tell her about the mess at my old job, but I didn't think we were quite there yet. We weren't even officially dating.

"Not today."

"Okay."

We continued upstairs, and my phone beeped. I pulled it out to make sure it wasn't work-related.

It was Travis.

> Travis: Want to meet for dinner tonight?

> Me: Sure. Where?

> Travis: Sydney said to invite Lydia. I told her to quit trying to set the two of you up.

> Me: LOL. Who knows? Maybe I'll ask her. But where are we eating?

> Travis: Can I let you know in a bit? Unless you have a preference?

> Me: Nope. Don't care as long as the food is good.

> Travis: I'll let you know soon.

I darkened my screen and put my phone back in my shorts.

"Good news?"

"Huh?" I asked.

"You're smiling."

I supposed I was. "It was Travis. We're going out for dinner."

"Sounds fun."

"He also said to invite you."

Her face brightened. "Really? That's so sweet. I did have fun with your friends the last time we were out."

"So, does that mean you want to come?"

"Sure. I didn't really have any plans anyway. I was going to maybe stop by my dad and stepmom's, but it wasn't set in stone. I didn't even tell them I was planning to go."

We reached my door.

"Great. Sydney will be happy. Travis said she's trying to set us up." I snagged her around the waist and kissed her. "Little do they know, we're already sleeping together."

Lydia put her hands on my forearms, and I couldn't help but notice how serious her face was. "Uh…"

"Oh shit."

"No, no, no. It's not bad. I just thought you and I were on the same wavelength."

I stepped back. "And that would be?"

"I don't really do relationships. Don't get me wrong. I love having sex with you and hanging out. I'm just not big on labels." She rolled her eyes. "I sound like an ass."

"No, you don't." I had once been the type of person who didn't like labels or to get serious either. But I had grown in the last few years. "I understand."

She looked relieved. "You do?"

"Yes. We'll just tell Sydney to mind her own business."

She frowned. "That seems a little harsh."

"That was a joke."

She laughed.

"But seriously, we don't have to tell my friends anything. You're my neighbor, and I'm training you. What we do in the privacy of our bedrooms is our business, not theirs." I smiled and wiggled my eyebrows. "Just as long as we get to keep doing that private business stuff." I grabbed her again and kissed her neck. "Because I'm not full of you yet."

She shuddered. "I'm not full of you yet either." She nuzzled behind my ear. "When is your first client?"

I looked at my watch. "In about ten minutes."

She gripped my sides. "I know you have the stamina of a stallion, but do you think you have it in you to have a quickie?"

I groaned. "This isn't fair."

She pulled my earlobe into her mouth.

"Okay, fine. But we'd better go to your place so that Rose doesn't think we were fucking when she gets here. I'll do the walk of shame."

Lydia pulled me toward her apartment and led me inside. As soon as the door closed, my mouth was on hers.

"We don't have time for kissing."

"Right." But I still kissed her as I guided her over to the kitchen counter. "One quickie, coming right up."

I spun her around and nudged her to lean over. I pulled down her pants and quickly grabbed the condom I kept in my pocket.

She turned her head at the sound of the packet ripping. "Did you have a condom on you?" she asked with a laugh.

"Yes. Try as I might to keep my hands off you while I'm working, I want to be prepared in case I can't."

She wiggled her ass. "I like a man who's prepared."

I lined up my cock with her pussy and thrust inside. "Thank God, because I don't want to stop now."

## TWENTY-SEVEN

# LYDIA

A WEEK LATER, I sat down at my computer to work.

It was the end of my third week of training, and I couldn't believe how much better I was getting at working out. I still didn't like it, but I was improving.

And today, I had to write my fourth article. It was hard to make them not feel the same and mundane. I was very thankful I only had to do them once a week. I did not understand how Hayley kept it exciting.

Since it was my least favorite thing to do for work, I wrote up my article first to get it over with. I mentioned Broderick and his training in there, and I reread everything three times to make sure that it didn't sound like I was involved with him. Because it was hard.

He was a great trainer, and I wasn't just saying that because I was sleeping with him. He pushed me when I needed it, but he understood that me and my body had limits. He never made me feel bad for not doing something.

We'd been working on swimming, and he never laughed at me for not really knowing how to swim. I had gone to the pool when I was a kid, but I never took actual lessons. I didn't really need to. I knew how to float and doggy-paddle, and I wasn't planning on going out for the swim team. But he'd taught me to do the front crawl, as it would help me go faster in the pool than simply doggy-paddling. I wasn't very fast yet, but I was learning.

I put this particular information in my article, but I left out the part where he made me feel safe and secure.

*Ugh.*

Despite telling him last week that I didn't want to get serious, I thought I was falling for Broderick. It was a good thing he had agreed with me about keeping our relationship as it was.

After completing Track Lydia, I moved on to Ask Lydia. I had gotten behind the last few weeks with my new responsibilities, so I was a couple days out with answering my emails. But part of that was also all the women writing in, wanting to get Guy Problems's information. I'd tried emailing back the first fifteen or so to tell them I didn't have that info because that was not how the system worked. Which they should have known because they had filled out the anonymous form. But alas, they didn't get it, and I soon realized that I was wasting too much time, especially when the emails kept coming.

I'd asked Eve to put a disclaimer in the magazine, but she was afraid it would hurt sales.

"Let them think they have a chance," she'd said.

*Whatever.* It was her magazine.

Today, I went through the obvious emails, asking for Guy Problems's info, and deleted them right away. And then

I went to work, hoping to respond to a lot of the questions in my inbox.

I was almost done for the day when I realized Guy Problems had written me again.

I was both a little excited—even though now it felt like I was kind of cheating on Broderick every time I got an email—and bummed. I didn't want Eve to exploit Guy Problems any further. I hadn't heard from him in a couple of weeks, and my boss had brought him up at the last two meetings, as if I could control when he wrote in. I felt bad because he was a real person with real concerns.

With really no other choice, I clicked on the message.

*Dear Lydia,*

*A friend informed me that there were many comments under my questions. Truthfully, I usually just go in to see what you have written back, but today, I thought I would see what other people had said.*

*One of the biggest questions is, am I still involved with my neighbor? And the answer is, I am. But I don't want to monopolize your advice column, so I am writing in today with a new concern.*

*For many years, I was probably what you would consider a serial dater. I dated women, but I never let it get to the serious stage. But as I've gotten older and grown, I have found that I don't want to be in one casual relationship after another for the rest of my life.*

*Now, I'm not saying I'm in love with my neighbor or anything because it's too soon for that, but I have discovered that I could see us getting serious. And wouldn't you know? She's the one who doesn't want to get too serious with me. I think this is Karma for all the women I pushed away in the past, or the universe is playing a joke on me.*

*What should I do? I don't want to pressure anyone to be in a relationship they don't want to be in, but I don't want to get my heart broken either. Should I wait to see where my neighbor and I are going, or should I break things off with her now?*

*Sincerely,*

*Guy Problems*

I sat back in my chair so hard that it squeaked. Eve and the readers were going to eat this shit up. I could just imagine all the women who would want to mend his broken heart.

I also noticed that he hadn't mentioned talking to his neighbor about the rumors. Had he finally talked to her? Was it all made up because it was really Broderick?

The similarities were so uncanny. Except Broderick had never said he wanted to get serious with me when I talked to him last week. He had seemed to agree with me.

I needed to stop overthinking this whole situation. It made sense that Guy Problems's relationship would naturally evolve, like mine had with Broderick. We just happened to have started at the same time. I just hoped his neighbor didn't actually break his heart. The readers were going to go wild if he wrote in and said he was single.

On that note, I wrote my response.

*Dear Guy Problems,*

*Every relationship and every person in a relationship is differ-*

ent. *Just because someone says they don't want to be serious, it does not mean they will always feel that way.*

*the key is not to rush anything. The worst thing you can do with someone like your neighbor is rush things. You will push her away.*

*Right now is the time to enjoy each other. Get to know each other. Don't push, but maybe you can talk about why she doesn't like to get serious. Perhaps it's something you can work on together. If she is open and willing.*

*And you are right in the fact that she might never want to be your girlfriend or get married. But it is too soon to tell. And yes, you might end up with a broken heart, but that's the risk in any relationship. I wouldn't throw something good away for a what-if.*

*Please know that I hope things work out for the two of you, but if they don't, I promise the ache you feel won't last forever, and you will move on. The heart can feel tremendous joy and a tremendous amount of pain. But it also has a tremendous capacity to heal. You might hurt for a while, but you will find someone new who will love to be in a relationship with you.*

*Wishing you all the luck,*

*Lydia*

## TWENTY-EIGHT

## BRODERICK

MY WATCH BEEPED, and I yelled, "Time."

Lydia and I both stopped running and settled into a brisk walk instead.

"I'm really proud of you," I told her. "You've come a long way since we began your training."

"Thanks. Before I started, I read that a person should train for eight to twelve weeks, so I guess nine isn't that bad."

Of course, the more training, the better, but I wasn't worried about her.

I picked up her hand and squeezed it. "You're going to do great. Don't worry about your time. Just concentrate on finishing."

She smiled. "I know."

It wasn't the first time I had given her that advice.

We had slowly gone faster and farther as the weeks went by. We now made it as far as the local park.

"Do you want to sit for a minute? I think we've earned it."

"Yes, please. When we started all this training, it wasn't so hot in the morning."

"I think the heat is more you than from the temperature outside."

She looked at me and wiggled her eyebrows. "Are you flirting with me, Mr. DeVries?"

I laughed. "You know I would never miss a chance to do that, but in this case, I'm not. You'll feel less overheated once we rest for a bit."

We found a bench and relaxed. We were still training early in the morning, so the park wasn't busy. A few people walking their dogs or jogging passed by us.

"I was thinking since next weekend is the event, we should do something this coming weekend to celebrate you making it this far." I couldn't believe how fast time had gone by and that the triathlon was less than two weeks away.

Her brow furrowed. "Shouldn't we do that *after* I complete the triathlon?"

I rested my arms on the back of the bench. "Nah. Too much pressure to finish." I met her eyes. "Because no matter what your bitch of a boss says, you don't have to go through with the whole thing. All you promised is that you would try."

Lydia laughed. "Damn, you're sneaky."

I shrugged. "Just telling it the way it is. If you put too much pressure on yourself, it's going to affect your blood pressure, your heart rate, your muscles. I know this whole thing isn't fun for you, but you can make it less stressful."

"You're so wise," she teased me.

"Nah. I just hate your boss and think you deserve better."

She laughed, and I couldn't help but smile. I loved making her happy.

"Anyway, you deserve to let loose and have some fun."

"I have fun with you every night, staying in."

I grinned. "That you do, but I was thinking about maybe inviting your friends."

"So, you're saying, you want to have an orgy."

I knocked my leg against hers. "You're such a dork. You know what I mean."

"What would we do?"

"Whatever you want. It's your celebration."

"What about if I want to go to a movie?"

"Then, we'll go to a movie."

"Even if you have to sit there for two hours?"

I laughed. "I like to work out, Lydia, but it doesn't mean I don't like relaxing too. We have watched movies together before."

She held up a finger. "But never in a movie theater, and we've never made it through one without making out, which usually ends up in sex."

"Believe it or not, I can control myself in public even if you are hard to resist."

She nodded slowly. "I'll think about it. Despite me giving you crap, I'm not sure that's what I want to do."

"It's Monday. You have all week."

She grabbed my arm, put it around her neck, and put her head on my shoulder.

I kissed the top of her head and breathed in her scent.

I loved that she wasn't afraid to snuggle up against me in public, but I made sure to never make a big deal of it.

I had read Lydia's advice to Guy Problems all those

weeks ago and was following it. But I knew I would have to come clean with her soon. Next week would be our last week training together, and for some reason, it felt like our relationship had an expiration date.

When we saw each other every day, it was a lot harder for her to push me away, in fear of getting serious. But once I no longer trained her every morning, it would be a lot easier for us to go back to being just neighbors.

And while I didn't want to push her into being my girl-friend or anything, I knew it was time to tell her I was the man behind the emails. I couldn't go on lying to her forever, and if she was going to hate me for keeping it a secret, then at least I would know I had come clean and let her know how I really felt.

"Do you think we should celebrate on Friday or Satur-day?" she asked me.

"I think Saturday. If we go out and party all night, then you can sleep in on Sunday."

She snorted. "I don't sleep in anymore, thanks to you."

"There, there. Once you're done training, you can sleep in again."

"I can't wait."

I tried not to flinch. In my head, I knew she was talking about sleeping. But in my heart, I took it as more than that. I wondered if she would miss seeing me every morning.

I supposed I was about to find out soon. I didn't want to ruin her celebration night, and I didn't want to tell her I was Guy Problems before a workout.

"What are you doing on Sunday?"

"Sleeping in," she joked.

"Besides that."

"Why do you ask?"

"Can we have lunch together?"

She sat up and tilted her head.

"What?" I asked.

She shook her head. "Nothing. It's just that we always play things by ear. I was wondering why you'd want to make a lunch date almost a week in advance."

I scrambled to come up with a good reason. "It's the last day before the triathlon that we both have off. We haven't talked about upping your training at all the last week, but we might want to. I want us to have lunch and not worry about any of that."

She leaned forward and kissed me. "It sounds like a date."

I pulled her close again for another kiss because I didn't want her to see how excited I was that she had called it a date.

## TWENTY-NINE

## LYDIA

PHOEBE KNOCKED her hip into mine. "Hey, girl, enjoying your party?"

I looked around and smiled at my friend. "Yes. Thank you for throwing a last-minute get-together for me."

Phoebe had been kind enough to host my celebration get-together for me at her place.

"Hey, you've earned it. You've worked really hard."

I took a sip of my drink. "Thank you. I have to admit, I feel pretty good about the whole thing. I made some extra money, and the readers actually seem to be liking my articles. I even had a couple people who had never read me before asking for advice."

"That's great." She threw her hair over her shoulder. "I mean, us gorgeous people need advice too," she said in a fake posh accent.

I couldn't help but laugh at her.

"How has your boss been? Does she worship at your feet for the favor you're doing her?"

I snorted. "She would never even admit that I am

helping her out." I shrugged. "She's been okay, especially since Guy Problems wrote in again. For some reason, she seems to think I can control when he asks for advice."

"So, the same bitchy person as ever."

"Yeah."

"Have you ever thought about quitting?"

"Yes, but besides her, I love my job. Can I just get a new boss instead?"

"Could you imagine if that were possible? If people could get rid of their horrible bosses, turnover rates in some places would go way down."

I stared off into space. "If only."

Phoebe laughed. "You could always start your own magazine."

I had just taken another drink and almost spit it out at her suggestion. "No way. Way too much responsibility. I have no connections, and I'd have to use all my savings on start-up costs. I'd rather go and work for the competition."

Phoebe pointed at me. "You should totally do that."

It was tempting. "With my luck, Eve's nemesis is a bigger bitch than she is."

Phoebe nodded to another part of the room. "How are things going with Broderick?"

"Good." I turned around to see him talking to my friend Gemma.

Their conversation looked completely casual. He was nodding at something she was saying, yet I couldn't help but feel a little jealous. Gemma was thin and pretty...and single.

"He and Gemma seem to be getting along well," Phoebe said.

"Why would you say something like that? Gemma is not a boyfriend thief."

Phoebe put her hands up in surrender. "Whoa, whoa, whoa. I just meant that he was getting along with your friends. It's a good thing. I hate dating guys who don't like my friends and vice versa."

I looked away sheepishly. "Sorry. I didn't mean to jump down your throat."

"It's okay. But you might want to take a hard look at a couple of things."

"What do you mean?"

She sighed. "If I spell it out for you, don't be mad at me, okay?"

I nodded.

"You like Broderick."

I raised my brow. "Well, duh. Otherwise, I wouldn't be having sex with him."

"No, I mean, you *like* him."

I still didn't get what she was hinting at. She wasn't very good at spelling things out.

"Okay, you're jealous."

"What? I am not."

"Yes, you are. Or you would have never said that Gemma wasn't a boyfriend thief. Also, the fact that you insinuated that he was your boyfriend is telling. No one can steal a boyfriend if he's not actually a boyfriend."

I frowned.

"But people also can't know to not 'steal' someone away if you don't make a relationship known." She swept her arm out. "How many people here know that you're sleeping together?"

I shrugged.

"It was a rhetorical question. You and I both know that probably only a tiny fraction of people here know that you're intimate with Broderick. Everyone else thinks he's your neighbor-slash-friend-slash-trainer."

I suddenly wasn't feeling so well.

It must have shown on my face because Phoebe cupped my elbow. "Hey, I'm not trying to upset you, but you can't have your cake and eat it too. You can't say he's not allowed to date anybody else yet not commit to him either. It's not fair to Broderick."

I was staring at Broderick, so she shook my arm.

"Before you panic, your relationship is still pretty new. I'm not saying you have to get married or anything right now. But at some point, you're either going to have to shit or get off the pot."

"You're full of metaphors tonight," I joked, mostly because I was trying to deflect my feelings.

She looked at me like I was a child she was disappointed in. "Just think about it, okay? What happens when he's not training you anymore? Have you guys even discussed if you're still going to see each other? Right now, you have an excuse, but what will happen when that's gone?" She let go of my arm and smiled. "And my metaphors are the shit."

I tried to smile back and set down my glass. "I think I'm going to go outside for a few minutes and get some fresh air."

I opted for the backyard and hoped that I would be alone. I didn't want to say hello or good-bye to anybody coming or going through the front.

I really hated that Phoebe was right, and the thought of

fully committing to Broderick had me panicking. But the thought of not seeing him anymore—or worse, seeing him with someone else—made me even more panicked. Which maybe told me something.

I sat and stewed in my thoughts for who knew how long when I heard some footsteps behind me.

"Hey."

I looked over my shoulder to see Broderick. I smiled. "Hey."

He sat down beside me. "Everything okay?"

"I was just thinking."

He put his arm around me and pulled me close. "Don't worry too much. You'll do great next Saturday."

I chuckled. I should've figured that he would think I was talking about the triathlon.

"You want to go home?" he asked me.

I knew that we were neighbors who lived in the same building, but I really liked hearing him say *home* as if we shared one.

I smiled. "Yeah."

## THIRTY

## BRODERICK

I FOLLOWED Lydia into her apartment. She didn't turn on the lights. She simply grabbed my hand and led me to her bedroom.

When we got there, I stopped before we made it to the bed and tugged her back toward me. "Are you okay?"

She smiled. "Yeah. Why do you ask?"

"First, you were sitting outside by yourself, and then you were quiet the whole way home."

She looked down.

I lifted her chin with a finger, so I could see her face again. "You know you can talk to me about anything. I know we didn't start out as the best of friends, but I care about you."

She fisted my shirt at my sides and dropped her head to my chest. "I care about you too."

"From your body language, I would say that isn't a good thing."

Her head flew up. "It's not. You weren't supposed to

make me like you so much. I liked being single. I liked having my life planned out."

I took her hand and walked us over to the bed, so we could sit. "I used to be like you."

"How so?"

"I didn't want to get serious. I liked doing things my own way, on my own time."

"So, what changed?"

"I would like to think that I matured, but it's more than that." I squeezed her hand. "There's something I should tell you that not many people know."

Her eyes grew round. She was probably imagining the worst.

"I tell a lot of people that I started working for myself because I wanted the freedom to do my own thing, but that is only partly true. Before I ventured out on my own, I worked at a big chain gym. I had worked there for quite some time and built up a good clientele. I actually had to cut off taking new clients because I just didn't have any more time in my schedule. But a friend of a client asked me for a favor, so I made an exception. This new client was nice and easy to work with. I noticed after a while that she did get a little bit of a crush on me, but I don't date clients."

"Is this why you asked me if you're my trainer who happens to be my neighbor or my neighbor who happens to be training me?"

"Yeah. There's just something about you I can't stay away from."

She smiled as her cheeks turned pink. She was adorable. "Continue with your story."

"She asked me out on a couple dates, and I politely declined. I thought that was the end of it. Until one day, the manager of the gym came to me and said that someone had made a complaint about me. I honestly had no clue because I tried to remain as professional as possible. I don't even touch my clients unless necessary, and when I have to, I make sure they're okay with it."

She squeezed my hand this time.

"So, I came to find out it was the new client. She said I had groped her breasts, that I'd tried to kiss her, and that I'd even followed her home once. As you can imagine, I was pissed as hell. The gym opened an investigation, and thankfully, there were cameras everywhere to check up on her claims. None of that stuff had happened, and the night I'd supposedly followed her home, I hadn't even been in the state."

"I'm so glad the truth came out."

"Yeah, well, she didn't care, and I think she wanted revenge for me turning her down. She told the gym that if they didn't fire me, she would go to the local news. Not the police because she knew she didn't have any proof, but the news. And sure, the news would have gotten the other side of the story, and I'm sure they would have reported that, too, but it would have been too late. The gym basically told me I had to quit or they were going to fire me."

"Oh, Broderick, that is awful."

"You're telling me. I actually think what the gym did to me was worse. I had worked there for years, and they just abandoned me like I meant nothing to them. I'd thought they'd disputed her claims to clear my name, but they had really done it to clear theirs."

Lydia scooted closer and wrapped her arms around me. "I'm sorry you had to go through that. Nobody deserves something like that."

I pulled us down to the bed, so we were facing each other. "Thank you. I wouldn't wish it on my worst enemy."

She cupped my face and brushed her lips over mine. "Thank you for trusting me with your trauma."

"Trust goes both ways. And if I want you to trust me, I have to trust you." I smiled. "Right?"

"Right." She took a deep breath while I held mine in hopes that she would tell me what was bothering her. "I really like you, but part of me is afraid of relationships."

"Oh, baby."

"I don't even have a traumatic story though. I've never really had my heart broken, and while my parents got divorced, they both remarried great people." She lifted a shoulder. "I don't know what I'm so afraid of."

"Just because nothing bad has ever happened to you doesn't mean you don't have the right to be afraid. Aren't you telling your readers all the time that they have the right to feel the way they feel?"

She grinned. "You read me?"

"Uh…" I sat up. "Since we're talking about trust, there's something else I need to tell you."

"Okay."

"I am Guy Problems," I confessed, and I waited for her to be upset since she had every right to be.

I wasn't prepared for her to start laughing.

She pumped her fist in the air. "I knew it!" She spread her arms out on the bed. "I feel so smart."

"Not to burst your bubble, babe, but I did talk about my neighbor."

She laughed again but quickly sat up, her face serious. "Wait. What did I ever say about you behind your back?"

"Something like you thought I was a jobless sex addict." I grinned at her.

Her whole face turned bright red. "So, Rose told you?"

"Oh, yeah."

"And you've been sitting on this information the whole time?"

"Eh, I thought it was kind of funny. And my ego kind of liked that you thought I could please that many women in one day," I teased.

She dropped her head in her hands. "I'm so embarrassed." Her head whipped up. "But in my defense, I didn't like you."

I gave her the side-eye. "But that's not really a defense."

"You're right. It's not. I think it actually makes me sound worse."

I pulled her toward me and kissed her. "Then, you're not mad at me?"

"No, I suspected the whole time." She bit her lip and grinned at me. "Plus, I've never had a guy write into an advice column and ask advice about me."

"That's because they're all fools."

"I really like you, Broderick," she whispered.

"I really like you too, Lydia. And maybe someday, you'll feel comfortable enough to be my girlfriend. But until then, I'm not going anywhere."

"I think that day is today." She looked up at me through her lashes. "If that's okay with you?"

"You don't have to ask me twice."

"Good. Now, give your girlfriend a kiss."

"Oh, I'm going to do much more than that," I promised and pulled her down to the bed once more.

# THIRTY-ONE

# LYDIA

IT WAS ANOTHER MONDAY, and I was sitting in front of my computer for our weekly meeting.

"Everyone," Eve said, "let's congratulate Lydia. She is on her final week of training, and Saturday is her triathlon event."

My coworkers all clapped for me.

"Thank you, but I will be happy when Hayley's leg heals, and she gets to do it next year. She is the one who deserves the applause."

"Thanks, Hayley," my coworkers said.

"I will be traveling to Minnesota. I'm going to meet with a couple people, and I thought I would check out Lydia in action," Eve announced, much to my chagrin. I did not want her at the event this weekend. "I leave Thursday, so we will be skipping our meeting that day. If anybody needs anything while I'm out of town, Sara is in charge."

Sara was Eve's right-hand woman and ran the show when Eve wasn't around.

"Lydia, have there been any other emails from Guy Problems?"

I was looking forward to telling Eve that she would never hear from Guy Problems again. A less mature part of me couldn't wait to see the disappointment on her face when she realized she couldn't cash in on him anymore.

"Actually, I have recently learned who Guy Problems is in real life. And I'm happy to report that his neighbor is now his girlfriend."

"Oh my God, who is he?" one of my coworkers asked eagerly.

A part of me knew to keep my mouth shut, but another part of me knew that stuff like this didn't come along every day, and I wanted to tell them the exciting news. In the end, I decided to not give too much away. "He's asked that I keep his identity private." Broderick hadn't exactly said that, but after what had happened to him, I felt it was safe to assume he would prefer it that way. "I'll just say that he is someone I know very well in real life." I decided to fib a little more to the story. "I guess he wasn't sure how to ask for advice in person, so that's why he went through the magazine."

I could practically see the wheels turning in all my coworkers' brains.

"You're such a tease."

"Is it your brother?"

"Is it your dad?"

"Is it an ex-boyfriend?"

"Is it your best friend who's secretly in love with you?"

"Someday, I'm going to get the info out of you."

I laughed at all the questions being thrown at me. "Both

179

my brother and my dad are happily married. It's not an ex-boyfriend or a best friend." I shrugged. "Sorry, ladies."

I noticed that while a lot of my coworkers had spoken up and seemed enthusiastic about the news, Eve hadn't said anything. I hadn't expected her to be happy, but I was shocked that she hadn't asked me a single thing. I began to mentally prepare myself for her to ask me to stay on the call after everyone else hung up.

She surprised me when she brought up advertising. "Lydia, your trainer still has one spot left for advertising. He only used one of the two I gave him. Do you want to ask him when he wants to use it?"

I frowned. Shouldn't she be asking him herself? Or even the person in charge of advertising? I looked at Niesha, and even though she couldn't be sure I was making eye contact with her, she shrugged. She didn't understand what Eve was talking about either.

Not wanting to give anything away about my relationship with Broderick, I said, "I can bring it up to him tomorrow at training. But if you need to know sooner than that, I would get ahold of him the way you did for the last spot he used."

"Niesha, can you do that, please?" Eve said.

"Will do," Niesha said.

"Thank you. Does anyone else have anything?" Eve asked.

After everyone said no, Eve went to end the call. "See you all next week. And I'll see you this weekend, Lydia."

And just like that, the meeting was over.

She hadn't asked me to talk privately. While I was relieved, I hoped she would leave me alone this weekend. I needed to concentrate on completing the triathlon, not worrying about my boss.

I picked up my phone.

> Me: Have you been having any trouble with the magazine and getting your advertising done?

About twenty minutes later, Broderick messaged me back.

> Broderick: No. The whole thing was super easy. Someone contacted me and asked what I wanted, and I told them. Next thing I knew, it was on the website. Why do you ask?

> Me: My boss brought it up at our meeting. It just seemed odd because that's not my department.

> Broderick: What did she say?

> Me: She asked me what you wanted to do with your last spot. I told her I would mention it at training tomorrow.

> Broderick: I'll let you know if I hear anything.

> Me: Thanks.

> Broderick: How did the rest of the meeting go?

> Me: I got to tell Eve that she wouldn't be hearing from Guy Problems anymore.

Broderick: Was she devastated?

Me: Not really. Which was kind of weird.

Broderick: Some people are just disappointing all around. They won't even let you ruin their day.

Me: LOL. Isn't that the truth? I remember one time when I was really little, I was mad at my mom. We had a dog, and he broke her favorite vase. I couldn't wait to tell her because I was a little shit. She just shrugged. That's it. I had wanted her to get mad.

Broderick: LOL. You should totally ask her about it now that you're both adults. She might have just been pretending it hadn't bothered her.

Me: *gasp* You might be right. I'm totally going to do that the next time I talk to her.

Broderick: My next client will be here soon, so I gotta go. I'll see you later?

Me: Yep.

I set my phone on my desk and went back to work. I noticed that I had an email from Eve.

*Lydia,*

*I would like to have dinner with you and your trainer on*

*Thursday when I'm in town. I want to discuss something regarding your assignment. Please see to the arrangements.*

    *Eve*


*What in the hell?* I didn't understand why she was doing this.

As soon as the triathlon was over, I wanted things to go back to the way they had been at work. I guessed there was no time like Thursday to let her know I wasn't doing any more special projects for her.

I needed to warn Broderick about the invitation.

## THIRTY-TWO

## LYDIA

MY KNEE BOUNCED up and down under the table as Broderick and I waited for Eve to show. She was late.

I squeezed his forearm. "Thank you for doing this. You could have said no."

He put his hand over mine. "I wouldn't let you face her alone."

The door to the restaurant opened, and I pulled my arm away. I stood to wave Eve over, but she'd already begun to make her way.

"Hello, Lydia," she said to me.

"Hello, Eve. You remember Broderick?"

Broderick stood and shook my boss's hand. "Hello, ma'am."

"Hello."

The three of us sat down, and our server came over to take our drink order. After she stepped away, we stared at our menus in silence.

It was going to be a long night if things stayed this awkward.

A few minutes later, Eve folded her menu. "I think I have decided."

As if our server was waiting for some kind of signal, she was back with our drinks and took our dinner order.

When we were alone again, Eve eyed Broderick and me over her glass of wine.

"So, Broderick, how long have you been a personal trainer?"

"Uh…" He looked away, as if he was doing the math in his head. "Almost ten years now."

Eve smiled. "That's great. Were you always Lydia's trainer?"

He smiled at me. "No. Just for this upcoming event."

"Oh? How did you two meet?" Eve asked a little too casually.

I didn't for one minute believe she was interested in the two of us.

"I'm Lydia's neighbor."

Eve took another sip of her wine. "That's kind of you to help her out."

I was done with the fake nice stuff.

"So, Eve, you said that you wanted to speak to the two of us about something."

"Ah, yes. I've noticed that you mention Broderick in some of the articles you've been submitting."

I hated that she made me feel like I had to justify my actions.

"He is my trainer, and I couldn't have trained without him. That was the whole point of the assignment."

"I'm not saying it's a bad thing."

Her tone a second ago had indicated it was.

"Anyway, many readers have connected with you, Lydia. They like that you're not a big fitness person. They can relate to you." She folded her hands and set them on the table. "I was hoping that after Saturday, you would continue to write monthly articles for the Fitness section." She looked at Broderick. "We will continue to pay his fees, of course."

I couldn't say no fast enough. "No, thank you. Whether I continue to work with a personal trainer or not, I want it to be on my own. The last two months have been a lot, and I feel as though Ask Lydia is starting to suffer. I don't want to do any extra assignments. At least, not for a while."

Eve shrugged. "Okay."

I frowned. "Really?" *Oops*. "I mean, you're okay with my decision?"

"Yes. You were hired for Ask Lydia, and that's all you are required to do."

I clenched my fist under the table. That wasn't what she had said at the beginning of this whole thing. She had black-mailed me.

Broderick grabbed my hand and squeezed.

I counted to ten before I said something I would regret. "I'm glad that's settled."

Eve looked over my shoulder. "Oh, here comes our food."

---

The next morning, I woke up in a bad mood. Even though Eve hadn't pushed her proposal on Broderick and me, I couldn't help but feel like the other shoe was about to drop.

I did not trust the woman.

The good news was that my anger at my boss really fueled my energy during my training.

"If you can stay this mad at your boss tomorrow, you'll do great," Broderick teased.

"Ha-ha. No, thank you. I don't want to be thinking about her at all."

"Good point." He kissed me on the lips and opened his apartment door. "Then, try not to stay angry, okay? She's not worth it."

"I'll try."

"Have a good day with work. I'll talk to you later."

I kissed him again and headed to my own place.

I took a shower and then started getting dressed when my phone rang.

It was Phoebe.

"Hey, girl. Shouldn't you be at work?"

"I am. But, Lydia, you need to go to your magazine website. Like, right now."

"Okay, hold on. I have to turn on my computer."

I hit the power button and sat down while I waited for it to start up.

"You want to tell me what this is about?" I asked my friend.

"I think you should just read it for yourself. My boss is staring at me, but call me if you need me."

A sense of dread washed over me.

"Okay." I hung up the phone and quickly went to *Afterglow*'s website.

The headline turned my blood ice-cold.

"Oh fuck."

# THIRTY-THREE

## BRODERICK

I WAS SETTING up for Rose when my phone rang. The caller ID said it was Travis.

"Hello?"

"What are you doing right now?"

I picked up a couple of weights and set them back on the rack. "Just getting ready for my first session. Why?"

"Sydney got a subscription to *Afterglow* after meeting Lydia, and I think you need to go and check the website."

"Okay."

"I'm really sorry, man."

Whatever had happened, it was not good.

I turned on my computer.

"Shit," Travis said. "Do you need Sydney's login info?"

"No, I have my own."

"Right. Of course you do."

I frowned. That was an odd thing to say. I didn't think it was that obvious that I subscribed to Lydia's magazine.

I found my laptop, typed in the website, and waited for it to load. What I saw there made my heart sink.

*Is our very own Ask Lydia basking in the afterglow of sex and love?*

*By Evelyn Gray*

And right underneath that was a picture of Lydia and me kissing. It was far away and looked like something a private detective would take, but you could still tell that it was the two of us.

"I have to go," I barely managed to say into the phone.

"Broderick, wait."

I hit End on my phone and let it fall to the floor.

*Fans of Ask Lydia and the new Track Lydia will be excited to discover that Lydia's personal trainer and our number one subscriber, Guy Problems, are one in the same. And I'm sorry, but it's time to move over, ladies, because this man is off the market. That's right. Lydia is Guy Problems's neighbor and his new girlfriend.*

I continued to read until I felt sick.

This couldn't be happening again.

There was a pounding at my door before it flung open, and Lydia ran inside. Her face was pale, and she looked distraught.

"Broderick—" She glanced over to my open computer. "You saw."

"Oh, yeah, I saw. What the hell happened, Lydia?"

"I don't know."

"How could you tell Eve about us after I told you what happened at my old job? Now, everyone is going to know I got involved with a client. I even Googled myself, and this disgusting article is the second thing that comes up after my website."

"I didn't tell her. All I said was that Guy Problems wouldn't be writing in anymore because I knew who it was and that it was someone close to me. She must have figured it out."

"Ya think?" I snapped.

She stepped forward and clenched her fists. "This is not my fault."

"From where I'm standing, it sure looks like you're the guilty party." I turned away from her. "I can't even talk to you right now."

She grabbed my arm. "Broderick, please. I'm sorry."

I just wanted her to leave me alone. I needed to figure out how I was going to fix this mess, and I couldn't do that with her around. Which was why I said the worst thing I could think of.

"Maybe you're right. Maybe you aren't relationship material." I pulled away from her and went to my bedroom.

A few seconds later, I heard my front door slam.

## THIRTY-FOUR

## LYDIA

I STOOD with the other contestants as we waited for the triathlon to start. "You haven't seen Broderick yet, have you?" I asked Phoebe.

She had come with me today to cheer me on, but I just wanted the whole thing to be over.

She shook her head sadly. "I'm sorry, I haven't."

Even with the way we had argued yesterday, I'd thought for sure he would still show up to support me today.

I felt like all the training I had done the last two months was for nothing. I had slept horribly last night, and all I wanted to do was bury my head under the covers.

"I still can't believe your boss wrote that article."

I looked at Phoebe. "Can we please not talk about her?"

"I'm sorry. I just wanted you to know I'm on your side." She narrowed her eyes. "And that she'd better not show her face here today."

"I know, and I think even Eve knows to stay away from me today." I hugged Phoebe. "Thanks for being here for me."

"Always." She stepped back and put her hands on my shoulders. "Remember, you can do this. And if you can't, that's okay too. Your boy—sorry. What I meant to say was, we're not going to let anyone get in the way."

Despite my sadness, I had to smile.

"I guess I'll see you at the finish line?" I asked hopefully.

"You're damn right you will."

---

Almost three hours later, I dragged my tired butt through the finish line. Broderick had been right. I didn't have the fastest time by a long shot. There were probably people who'd chosen the longer route and beaten me, but I'd made it through. And knowing I had done it felt pretty damn good.

I looked through the crowd in search of Phoebe.

When I heard a high-pitched, "Lydia," I had to smile.

Phoebe burst through the crowd with my parents, step-parents, and brother behind her. My family started clapping when they saw me.

My friend flung her arms around me and gave me a bear hug. "You did it."

My mom hugged me and kissed me on the cheek. "I'm so proud of you, honey."

Eli socked me in the arm and grinned. "Way to go, brat."

"Thanks, everyone, for being here."

My mom brushed her thumb over my cheek. "Oh, honey, you don't have to cry."

"I know." I waved my hands over my face. "It's just a lot of emotions, ya know?"

She rubbed my back. "I know."

"Should we go out and celebrate?" my dad asked.

"Oh, Dad, you're so sweet, but I am spent. I want to go home, put on my pajamas, and do nothing the rest of the night. In fact, I might have dinner delivered right to my couch."

Everyone laughed, and my dad hugged me. "How about tomorrow or next weekend then?"

"Sounds like a plan."

We walked to the parking area. My walk was actually more like limping because my muscles were so sore, but everyone else walked. And even though a special someone wasn't there, I still felt pretty darned loved.

My dad and stepmom's car was first, and we said good-bye. Phoebe's car was next, and since she was taking me home, I hugged my mom again and said good-bye to her, my stepdad, and my brother.

I was just about to get into the passenger seat when my dad came rushing over.

"Hey, honey. I forgot to give you this." He handed me a piece of paper.

"What is this?"

"When I stepped away from your brother and mom to find a restroom, some guy asked if I was your dad. He said to give it to you and that you would know what it was about." He kissed my cheek. "See you later."

"Bye, Dad."

After he walked away, I unfolded the paper.

*I knew you could do it.*
*Broderick*

I gasped. He had been here to see me after all.

"Are you getting in or what?" Phoebe called from the driver's side.

I collapsed into my seat and handed her the note.

She put it against her chest. "Aww…Lydia, he was here."

"I know."

She handed me back the paper. "So, what are you going to do?"

I clenched my jaw. "I'm not quite sure yet, but I'm not going to let Eve get away with what she did. She can't do what she wants with other people's lives."

Phoebe put her car in drive. "I can't wait to see what you come up with."

---

The next day, after sleeping a full ten hours last night, I woke up and started on my plan.

I finished my final article for Track Lydia and a special Ask Lydia question and answer, and then I called up Sara.

"Is Eve still out of town?"

"Yes. I saw the article. I can't believe she did that. She didn't even show it to me first."

I wouldn't have blamed Sara for not stopping Eve, but it was nice to know she was on my side.

"I was wondering if you would do me a favor."

"What is it?"

"I have a couple of things I'm going to send to your email because I don't trust the cloud. I would love it if you posted them in their entirety, but if you don't, I'll understand."

"Done."

"You haven't even read them yet."

"Don't have to. I'll do it."

I grinned. "Thank you, Sara."

"Can I ask a question?"

"Yes?"

"Are you going to stick it to Eve?"

"That's the goal."

She laughed. "I can't wait to see what you send me."

I hung up the phone. My next stop was *Captivate*'s website. There was a certain editor in chief I was hoping to speak with there.

## THIRTY-FIVE

## BRODERICK

MONDAY DIDN'T SEEM the same without my early morning training with Lydia. I missed her like crazy, and I was so proud of her for finishing the triathlon the way she had.

I had picked up my phone half a dozen times the day before to call her, but nothing I'd prepared to say sounded good enough. I knew I was going to have to see her sooner or later, but I couldn't seem to find the right words.

I had been fiddling with my phone all morning, too, wondering if I should chicken out and just send a text. But even then, I didn't know what to write.

My phone buzzed in my hand.

> Sydney: You need to check Afterglow's website again.

*Oh shit.*

> Sydney: It's good this time. I promise.

I sure hoped she was right.

Just like the other day, I pulled up the website and started reading. The first thing was Lydia's final article about her experience with training and participating in the event. The end was what really caught my attention.

My trainer, Broderick DeVries, was the best trainer anyone could ask for. He was kind and patient when I needed it, yet he knew when to push me too. I'd met him because we live in the same building, but it wasn't until my training that I really got to know him, and I'm so lucky that I did.

If you live in the Minneapolis area, you will not find anyone better than him. And if you don't live in the city, he offers online classes that you can do from the comfort of your living room.

But I wouldn't wait too long. I have every confidence that his schedule will fill up soon.

I smiled when I finished reading. I knew there was no way to undo the damage her boss had done, but letting the world know that I was good at my job was the best step she could have taken.

I was about to shut off my computer when I noticed a familiar name in the next section of Ask Lydia.

*Dear Lydia,*

*I used to think of myself as someone who didn't do relationships. I've been the single friend most of my life.*

*But recently, I have fallen in love with a wonderful guy. He is everything a woman could ask for in a man. He's sexy, kind, funny, and trustworthy. Don't get me wrong; he's not perfect. He doesn't like my cooking, and he likes to listen to his music too loud.*

*However, he's perfect for me.*

*Unfortunately, someone I trusted—and shouldn't have—used our relationship for their own personal gain, and it really hurt the man I love. I know I am partly to blame for his hurt and pain, and now, I don't know how to fix the situation. I'm afraid he'll never trust me again—with either his past or his heart.*

*Sincerely,*

*My Guy Problem*

I stopped breathing. This had to be Lydia. She had purposely used a name like mine. I couldn't wait to see if she had given herself advice.

*Dear My Guy Problem,*

*I'm sorry to hear that you went through this, and no one should ever abuse your relationship like that. Even if you trusted the wrong person, the blame is fully on that person. There is too much victim-blaming in this world. And you are a victim just as much as the man you love is.*

*My advice to you is to talk to him after you are both calm. Having a conversation when either of you is upset won't help the situation. Once the two of you are in a clearer frame of mind, reach out to him. Explain what happened. If he loves you, he will understand. If he continues to put the blame on you, then perhaps he's not the perfect man for you after all. No matter how much you love him, you have to make sure that he will never hold what happened against you. A relationship full of resentment is unhealthy.*

    *I wish you all the best.*

    *Sincerely,*

    *Lydia*

Even though she was talking to herself, I loved Lydia's advice because she was right. I scrolled a little bit further to see she had written something else.

*Dear Readers,*

    *Thank you for supporting me as your resident advice guru and recently as your floundering fitness novice. I have loved—almost —every minute of my job, but it is time for me to say good-bye. These are the last two articles I will write for Afterglow.*

    *I will miss you all and my wonderful coworkers.*

    *I couldn't have asked for a better job, and I hope to meet you again in my future endeavors.*

    *Sincerely,*

    *Lydia Karels*

I slammed my laptop closed, jumped up from my seat, and raced over to Lydia's.

I knocked on her door and started pacing, afraid she wouldn't answer.

"Broderick?"

I spun around to see her standing in her doorway—I

hadn't heard her open it—and I rushed over to her. I picked her up in my arms and hugged her close. Quickly, I carried her inside and shut the door.

As I set her on her feet, I asked, "Are you My Guy Problem?"

"You read that, huh?"

"Every word."

"Yes, it's me. I was hoping if I used a similar name, you'd figure it out."

I cupped the back of her head and kissed her until she was moaning.

I pulled away, and she opened her eyes with a sigh.

"Does this mean we're back together?" she asked.

I frowned. "We never broke up."

"But what about Friday?"

"We fought, Lydia. Couples do that. I needed some space, and after how cruel I was to you, I wanted to give you space too."

"Oh."

"You did get my note, right?"

She smiled. "I did. I just didn't know what it meant."

"It meant that even though I was upset, I would never miss your big day. Also, I'm sorry I said you weren't relationship material. There is no excuse for being so mean."

"I'm sorry about my boss."

"Don't you mean, ex-boss?"

She smiled. "Yes, ex-boss."

"She's a horrible person, but what she did was not your fault. I'm sorry I ever blamed you." This was the second thing I had to apologize for. "I love you, but I think advice from Ask Broderick would be to find someone who's not an ass to work for at your next job."

"You love me?"

I laughed. "I do."

"I love you too."

"I know," I joked. "You already put it online."

She laughed. "I guess I did."

"So, did you really quit your job?"

"Yes, and no. I haven't heard back from Eve yet."

"You mean, your letter to the readers is how you told your boss? How did that work?"

She grinned. "She was still out of town, so I asked the person in charge to publish my stuff."

"You are amazing."

"Thank you."

I kissed her. "I love you."

"I love you too. But just so we're clear, I'm never working out as much as you do."

I laughed. "I'd never expect anything less."

---

A month later, Lydia and I were cuddling on her couch, watching TV, when her phone rang.

She checked the caller ID. "Unknown number." She looked at me.

"Answer it."

Her hand was practically shaking. "Hello?" she answered.

A few seconds later, she turned around and mouthed, *It's her.*

I smiled. "Her" was the editor in chief of *Captivate*. Lydia had dipped into her savings the last month to pay her rent, so I knew how excited she was to hear from this magazine. And since the editor had taken the time to call, I had a good feeling that my girlfriend was about to land herself a new job.

# EPILOGUE
## LYDIA

A FEW YEARS LATER

I WENT to find Broderick downstairs in the basement. He was working out, but I needed to talk to him.

We'd been together two years now and recently bought our own house. It had taken a while, but I'd finally gotten my own place.

We'd had to wait longer than I had originally planned because after everything that happened at *Afterglow*, Broderick's popularity increased, and we both got weary of clients finding out where he lived. He actually got a couple of offers from local gyms, but we both decided that he liked being on his own too much. So, he rented his own space and filled it with all his equipment and then some. The wait had been worth it in order to get our own place.

And I was very happy, working at *Captivate*. Eve's nemesis and my new boss was great. Someday, I hoped to find out what had happened between the two of them, but I wasn't going to pry.

I leaned against the wall as I watched Broderick do squats. He still got me to do cardio a few days a week with him, but I was glad I didn't put my body through what he put his through.

As he watched his form in the big mirror on the wall, he caught me staring at him and smiled. He set his weights down. "Hey."

"Sorry. I didn't mean to make you stop."

He picked up the towel on his weight bench and wiped his face. "It's okay. Everything all right?"

I walked farther into the room. "Did you mean what you said? That you'd love me, no matter how big I got?"

He smiled. "Yes." He grabbed my hips and pulled me toward him. He rubbed his beard against my neck. "As long as you get good heart exercise and the doctor says your labs are within normal range, I'm happy." He pulled back. "Why do you ask?"

I ran my hands over his shoulders and down his arms. "It's funny that you mention labs because the doctor just called me with the results for one."

I could see the worry flash in his green eyes.

"Are you okay?"

"Yes, but I was thinking of finally taking you up on your offer."

He frowned. "Offer?"

"The offer to get married."

A grin slid over his face. Broderick had been wanting to get married for over a year, but he'd patiently been waiting for me to be ready too. "I am so confused. The doctor called today, and now, you want to get married. What kind of results did you get that would make you want to be my wife?"

I just smiled at him.

His eyes grew big as he looked down at my belly and back up to me. "No?"

I held up my hands. "Surprise."

He picked me up in my arms and spun me around.

"Whoa, whoa. You have to set me down before I get sick."

"Sorry." He put me back on my feet. "Is this for real?" he asked. "I'm not dreaming?"

"It's real. You're getting a wife and a baby."

He hugged me as his body shook with laughter. "This is the best day ever."

# MY COVER MODEL SAMPLE

## SYDNEY

The combined noise of two phone alarms with completely different songs woke us up at six fifteen the next morning.

I quickly shut mine off, as did Harper.

"That was a horrible noise," I commented from my bed.

"Yep, I'm up," Harper said. "Although I'm wondering now why we stayed up late, watching movies."

"I'm wondering whose idea it was to schedule a seven a.m. breakfast on a Saturday."

Harper sat up. "No kidding. It's my day to sleep in. What the hell, people?"

I pushed my covers off me and sat up as well. "We could always skip it?"

Harper's eyes widened. "And miss free food?"

"You're right. I don't think they have coffee though. We'll have to go and get one before."

Harper stood. "I'd better get ready then."

"Are you showering before you go?" I called out to her.

"No, I'm just going to get dressed and go. I'd rather shower after, so I can look pretty for the book signing."

"Thank God. I didn't want to shower either."

I spent most days sitting in front of my computer or running errands. Most of the time, I didn't even bother with makeup, doing my hair, or putting my contacts in. My outfit of choice was a T-shirt and yoga pants.

So, when it came to book signings, I always liked to look a little more professional. But I really didn't feel like doing all of that before seven in the morning if I didn't have to. Besides, I didn't have time.

I brushed my hair and my teeth and put my hair up in a ponytail. I put on clean clothes, and, yes, I decided to go with yoga pants because I wanted to be comfortable.

"We'd better go. I don't want to be one of the last ones there and have to sit with people we don't know."

"What's wrong with that?" Harper asked.

She could make friends with a wall.

"Nothing, except that I hate imposing on people." I grabbed my name tag and my key card.

"But you're an author. People want to meet you."

"I'm a non-famous author," I reminded her.

Harper grabbed her things and looped her arm with mine. "Then, let's go make them want to meet you."

We went and got large lattes first before we headed to the area where we were supposed to meet for breakfast. There weren't that many people around, but there also weren't many tables.

"See, it's a good thing we came early."

"Yeah, yeah," Harper said with a smile.

After the food was rolled out, we filled up our plates and

brought them back to our table. I wasn't a health food nut, but I did try to eat well most of the time to keep myself from gaining too much weight. But I was on vacation, and I was eating as much breakfast as I wanted.

"Oh my God," Harper said with a moan. "These are the best muffins."

"Crap. And I didn't get one."

She broke off a huge piece. "Here, try some."

I opened my mouth, intending to take a bite, but she shoved the whole thing in my mouth. Both of us started laughing, and I had to turn my face toward the wall behind me. If I kept looking at Harper, I wouldn't stop giggling, and I didn't want the room to stare at my chipmunk cheeks.

A close female voice said, "Do you mind if we take your other two chairs?"

Out of the corner of my eye, I saw Harper wave her arm at our empty chairs. "Go ahead. Those seats are free."

"Thank you," a male voice said.

I finally managed to chew half of the food in my mouth and swallow it. "You bitch," I told Harper as I turned around.

She laughed again, and I probably would have, too, except I was stopped dead when I saw who was about to take the seat across from me.

It was Travis Zehler, and holy shit, but the few pictures I had seen online did nothing to prepare me for him in real life.

He was tall with broad shoulders and a trim waist, and when he turned to point to something, talking to the woman beside him, I noticed he had a gorgeous ass, too. I wouldn't have even needed to look up his picture to know this was him. He carried himself in such a way that there was no other word for it than modelesque.

Now, I remembered how I'd thought he wasn't the cutest guy I'd ever seen. His hair was shorter than the few pictures I'd seen, and he had a trim beard. When he smiled at us, I knew I wanted to have his babies.

*Why did I decide not to look pretty this morning again?*

Harper kicked me under the table, and I realized I'd been staring. With my mouth open. With food in it.

Travis shook his head and laughed.

I was going to kill Harper later.

The woman to my right had on a purple name tag like me and was probably about my age. She had shoulder-length auburn hair and pretty brown eyes. "Hi, I'm Angela Devlin."

I swallowed my food, composed myself, and smiled. "I'm Sydney Hart." I'd seen her name around on social media, but I hadn't read any of her books yet.

"I'm Harper, I'm Sydney's assistant."

"This is Travis," Angela said, pointing to him. "He's my assistant-slash-model."

"So, when did you two get in?" Harper asked. "We saw your name tag still on the table last night," she said to Travis.

He smiled, but Angela was the one who said, "We got here about midnight."

Harper winced. "Ouch. And you both got up so early?"

"I slept almost the whole way here from Minneapolis, so I had plenty of rest. But I did just throw on some clothes this morning," Angela said.

"Us, too," I said with a laugh. "That's where we're both from."

Although Travis looked great for someone who had driven for hours and gotten no more than six hours of sleep.

"Are you both from Minneapolis?" I asked. I thought I had read Travis was from somewhere farther away, but maybe I was wrong. I hadn't given his bio my full attention the night I looked him up.

"I'm from Michigan," Angela said. "I flew into Minneapolis and drove here with Travis."

"But you're from Minnesota?" I asked Travis.

"Yep. Born and raised." He grinned, and not one, but two dimples appeared. *Figures.* "I grew up in a small town, moved to the Cities in high school, and stayed."

I couldn't believe he was from the same place I lived. Despite just meeting him, he gave off this aura. I didn't know how to explain it, and it was kind of like finding out a famous actor lived near me.

"That's so cool that you decided to attend," Harper said.

"Yeah, Ang convinced me," he said, and I noticed the nickname he used for her. They must be close.

"How did you do that?" I asked Angela, half-joking, half-serious. "I think he's the only model to attend this weekend."

She laughed. "I did a lot of begging and pleading."

Travis shook his head, but he was smiling.

"Truthfully, he's just a really nice guy."

Travis shook his head again, and mouthed, *No, I'm not.*

Harper and I both laughed.

Angela put her hand up to her mouth, so Travis couldn't

see what she was saying, but then she proceeded to speak loud enough for him to hear. "He's also a big softy."

"Shh...don't tell anyone." Travis shoved a forkful of food in his mouth and grinned.

I mentally sighed. *God, he's beautiful.*

Harper leaned over to me and whispered, "Just a guy, huh?"

# ABOUT THE AUTHOR

R.L. Kenderson is two best friends writing under one name.

Renae has always loved reading, and in third grade, she wrote her first poem where she learned she might have a knack for this writing thing. Lara remembers sneaking her grandmother's Harlequin novels when she was probably too young to be reading them, and since then, she knew she wanted to write her own.

When they met in college, they bonded over their love of reading and the TV show *Charmed*. What really spiced up their friendship was when Lara introduced Renae to romance novels. When they discovered their first vampire romance, they knew there would always be a special place in their hearts for paranormal romance. After being unable to find certain storylines and characteristics they wanted to read about in the hundreds of books they consumed, they decided to write their own.

One lives in the Minneapolis-St. Paul area and the other in the Kansas City area where they both work in the medical field during the day and a sexy author by night. They communicate through phone, email, and whole lot of messaging.

You can find them at http://www.rlkenderson.com, Facebook, Instagram, TikTok, and Goodreads. Join their reader group! Or you can email them at <u>rlkenderson@</u> <u>rlkenderson.com,</u> or sign up for their newsletter. They always love hearing from their readers.

www.ingramcontent.com/pod-product-compliance
Lightning Source LLC
Chambersburg PA
CBHW060922180626
46817CB00004B/1355